SECOND

Semester

A
CAMPUS
TALES STORY

Q.B. TYLER

Cover Design: NET Hook & Line Designs
Editing: Kristen—Your Editing Lounge
Interior Formatting: Champagne Book Design

"Take a lover who looks at you like maybe you are magic."
—Frida Kahlo

SECOND
Semester

One

Landon

HUNGRY GREEN EYES WITH TRACES OF GOLD LOOK UP FROM between my legs. Eyes that tell me everything I already know about the person behind.

I know the type.

Daddy issues. A wealth of them.

A girl that wants a man who will give her the love and affection that she didn't get from her father. A man that will let her sit on his lap, call her princess, and five minutes later spank her pretty little ass pink.

I run my hand through the hair of the green-eyed goddess in front of me and pull at the wild curly brown locks that I'd long released from the confines of the bun at the nape of her neck.

The gold flecks in her eyes reflect off my Rolex and I watch them widen at the watch that I'm sure she knows it costs more than her salary.

Her eyes flit back to me before fluttering closed as she continues to take me in her mouth and force my dick down her throat. She sputters and chokes slightly as she goes too far and my dick hardens more in appreciation as drool forms at the corners of her mouth.

"You're such a pretty little doll, aren't you? Are you going to be a good girl and make me come?" She nods, giving me a look that tells me she's dying for my praise. Eyes that bore into mine and practically beg for me to tell her that she's doing a good job. I grip her face pushing my dick further and harder into her mouth and I watch as the tears form in her eyes and run down her cheeks. Streaks of black trickle down her ivory skin and hit the hardwood floor of my office.

But she doesn't let up. Years of feeling like she'd let her father down. Feelings that told her she wasn't good enough and that she would never be good enough push her forward, determined to make me come.

Preston will kill me when he finds out that I've fucked yet another one of his paralegals. But honestly, he had only himself to blame. *Stop hiring highly fuckable women. You know I'm a man going through a brutal divorce.*

I grunt, thinking about my soon to be ex-wife, Jana Fucking West. The mother of my son and also the devil in disguise. My phone beeps, and I welcome the distraction from thinking about the woman who is gunning for half of my money and even more than half of all my properties.

P. Mitchell: Be there in ten.

"Fuck." I groan. "If you even have a prayer at getting off, I'd work quicker. I need you out of here in eight and a half minutes."

I feel her lip tremble slightly under my dick before she lets it slide out of her mouth. I shoot her a look, wondering what exactly she thinks she's doing. "Can't we just have sex?" I glower at her, wanting her to feel the heat of my disappointment, and I see her eyes preparing to backtrack. "I just mean…"

"Let me get this straight," I rub my cock from root to tip in front of her face. "You tease me for the entire length of this morning's meeting, running that sinful tongue all over that goddamn pen. You send me the obscenest texts last night when you were out with your friends of just what you wanted to do with my dick today, and now…you're backing out?"

"I'm not, I just…"

"Oh, *Olivia*." I emphasize her full name and I watch as she shrinks beneath my gaze. I usually call her Liv or Livi like everyone, but I use Olivia to be a dick. To remind her of the other man who called her that.

Her eyes well up with tears as she stands and straightens her navy pencil skirt. "I'm done with this. This isn't good for me." I blink, preparing for the inevitable tantrum that is just moments away. "You're cold and hurtful and…"

"But I eat your pussy better than anyone ever will. You're not going anywhere, pretty girl. You're addicted to this. To how I make you feel. To how *this* makes you feel. I've ruined you for other men, Olivia, and you know it."

She tucks an errant curl behind her ear and looks at the floor, unable to meet my gaze. "You're married."

My heart has been enclosed in a block of ice for what seems like a full year, and Olivia seems to be wielding an ice pick. *Do not go down this road with disposable pussy, West.* "I'm separated, which you know, so I'm failing to see your point."

"I work here. This is against the no-fraternization policy."

"Cute." I pull my pants up, realizing that my best friend and partner will be walking through my door in less than five minutes and there was no chance I'd be coming before then. I straighten my tie and fiddle with my cufflinks to ignore her imploring eyes.

"I'll sue for…sexual harassment."

3

My blood runs cold and a chill slithers down my spine. But then I remember who the fuck I am: a ruthless lawyer with an axe to grind with a large number of the female population having been burned by one and feeling the need to take it out on the rest of them. *Call her fucking bluff.*

"You'd do that?"

She's silent, and I know I've got her. Olivia may be pissed, but she wouldn't do that. Not when she was the one that came to me. Not when she was the one to initiate the first interaction. Girls like Olivia thrived on men with power. They wanted in, no matter what it took. Too bad all the women want Preston at first. And Preston Mitchell, who has been hopelessly in love with his wife since the moment he'd laid eyes on her, is never going to fucking stray.

They want the hero they can't have.

So, they come to me and it made me realize that they don't *really* want the hero.

They wanted the villain.

I'm not respectful. I don't open doors or send *good morning* texts. I fuck them rough and hard and make them come so many times they often pass out from the pleasure.

And the rate in which they come back for *seconds* and *thirds* and *fourths* does nothing but convince me that women don't want the hero. *They want the villain.*

I take a step towards Olivia and begin to re-button the blouse that I'd torn open in my haste to get her pert nipples in my mouth. "You'd really say I forced myself on you? That I did something you didn't want…that you didn't *beg* for? That I initiated this whole thing?" *I was a lot of things, but I'd never touch a woman who didn't want it. This was just a bitch looking for a payout.*

"I…"

Two raps on the door, followed by Preston walking through, stops her from speaking. His phone is glued to his ear, giving me a chance to take a long look at who follows him into the room: a petite, slender brunette that my dick responds to before my brain can even tell it to abort mission. My eyes trail up her body, long toned legs accentuated by pumps and a pair of perfectly tailored gray slacks that I briefly wonder what would look like on the floor of my office. A white silk blouse is tucked into her pants with a jacket that matches her pants over it. Her hair is pulled back off of her face, allowing me to see perfectly flawless, tanned skin and hazel eyes accentuated by thick-rimmed, square glasses. She looks like a fucking pinup girl. A sexy librarian.

No.

She looks like someone who shares Preston Mitchell's DNA.

Fuck. Serena?

I blink away from her, grateful that Preston is still on the phone and unbeknownst to the fact that I was just ogling his oldest daughter. But then I remember there is someone else in the room, and the way she's looking at me, it seems *she has* noticed.

Olivia tucks a hair behind her ear and raises an eyebrow full of judgment and, if my intuition is correct—which it usually is—a hint of jealousy as well. "Is there a reason you're still here?" I narrow my gaze at her and she turns her face towards Preston to avoid further embarrassment, though I can see the flush creeping up her neck.

"Yes, I'll be there in twenty." I hear Preston end his call and turn to me and Olivia. "Miss Barrett?" He gives me a disapproving glare, masquerading as a joke. "Landon, what did I tell you about abusing my paralegals. You have your own." He

5

chuckles, though I can hear the nervousness in his voice. *He's going to chew you out, West.*

She clears her throat and nods slightly. "Mr. Mitchell."

"I left a few things on your desk for you. I'm due in court in twenty, do you think you have time to type a quick memo?" he asks her. That's one thing about Preston Mitchell. He asks. I demand. He treats his interns the same way, and they are never prepared when they leave our firm. Mine, on the other hand, go on to take over the world with stellar recommendations from me. My last one, who just left for Stanford Law last week, emails me updates every two weeks. I can't wait to hire her ass the second she gets out of law school.

Thank God, I didn't fuck that one.

"Yes, of course, Mr. Mitchell. I'll be right on it." Olivia flees from the room as if she's on fire and closes the door. Just as she does my best friend glares at me.

"I will fucking kill you," Preston growls.

I hear a gasp from the corner of the room. A gasp under normal circumstances I wouldn't have heard. But I am acutely aware of the gorgeous proverbial elephant in the room and I've made note of every movement she's made since she's walked through the door.

I swear to God, if she fiddles with her glasses just one more time.

"She's the best paralegal I've ever had. Can't you keep it in your pants for one goddamn minute!?" he snaps.

I'd met Serena Mitchell before. She was the older more reserved sister, very unlike her sister Skyler, who Preston is ready to go into an early grave over.

Thank God, I don't have a daughter.

Although, I'd met Serena a few times in passing, I hadn't remembered her looking quite like this.

"It's a pleasure to see you again, Serena." I take a few steps and reach for her hand. She swallows and touches her glasses again, pushing them further up her face.

"Mr. West."

"Landon." I give her a warm smile, probably the most genuine one I'm capable of. Not the one I use when I want in a woman's panties, but the one I use when I'm talking to Griff, the boy who shares *my* DNA but also as of lately, hates my guts.

My heart squeezes slightly, the ice cracking in my chest as I think about my sixteen year old son who blames me for everything. A son who is currently dealing with the ramifications of a DUI, more than likely as a result of the divorce his mother and I are going through. A DUI that is also somehow my fault according to his mother.

"Would you mind if I spoke with your father for a moment, *alone?*"

Preston, who must have remembered that his daughter was in the room turns to look at her. "I'm sorry you had to hear that, Rena, can you go wait in my office?" He winces, probably feeling horrible that his twenty-one year old daughter heard him swear. I swear he coddles the shit out of them both. Skyler is a firecracker who can take care of herself; I could see that the moment I met her, in addition to what her parents had told me. But this one: *Serena.* She is sensitive and innocent. And those wide bright eyes behind her glasses...

Fuck, they haven't seen anything yet.

The need to shelter her from all the bad shit in the world comes at me in full force, and suddenly, I have a moment of clarity that rocks me to my core.

I am the bad shit in the world.

Two

Serena

I FLEE FROM THE ROOM NOT WANTING TO BE IN THAT ENCLOSED space with all that tension. Tension between my father and Landon West and whatever was leftover between Landon and that pretty paralegal. I could sense the frost in the air as I walked into the room and the way he avoided her gaze while she all but stared at him with stars in her eyes makes me wonder what happened between them before we entered. My father was on the phone, but I had noticed the awkwardness almost instantly. *Was this Mr. West's—er, Landon's girlfriend?* I remember reading in the firm policy that fraternization of any kind is strictly prohibited. *No exceptions.* And being a partner at the law firm, I have to assume that he abides by those rules, right?

But I certainly didn't miss the way my skin tingled when I looked at him. Goosebumps shot up all over my arms and I had never been more grateful for the blazer covering my physiological reaction to this GQ model disguised as a lawyer. His perfectly angled jaw, that looked like it could cut glass, was covered with a smattering of dark stubble. His eyes were dark and brooding, with an icy tint, although they softened dramatically when they met mine. And when I met his gaze, he looked almost sad, and I felt the pull to hold him in my arms and remove that expression from his face. He was beautiful. The most beautiful man I'd ever seen, so I averted my gaze.

Because he isn't mine to look at.

I walk down the long hallway, away from Landon's office towards my father's, my heels clicking against the dark, shiny hardwoods and echoing off the walls. I pass awards, accolades, and magazine and newspaper clippings hanging in gold frames acknowledging the "excellence" of the firm. I stop at the one right outside my father's office that highlights a case he recently won. *The Heart of Hartford,* the article was titled. I beam with pride as I run my fingers over the picture that speaks of my father's heartfelt closing remarks.

"So, you're going to be helping out around here?" I turn and spot Olivia, the source of the voice that is laced with judgment and annoyance.

"Yes." I nod and swallow hard, my nerves kicking into high gear as I can already tell this girl doesn't like me very much. I'm far from shy when I'm in my own element, and right now, I am far from that. Besides, this is an adult. Like a real adult. Not the "I'm over twenty-one and while I can legally drink, I still need my mother to make my dentist appointments" type adult. No, this was the kind of adult that paid bills and taxes and wasn't currently on their parents' health insurance.

"I'm your father's paralegal and, as someone who's been here a while and seen quite a bit, can I give you some advice?"

With a 4.0 GPA and a double major in writing and rhetoric alongside my rigorous pre-law major, I know a rhetorical question when I hear it. I don't bother responding; I simply blink at her, willing her to go on with her "advice" that more than likely is along the lines of *"I don't care who your daddy is, stay out of my way and keep your eyes off of my man."*

9

She looks me up and down and I take a moment to do the same. Her skirt is far too short, her top is a bit too tight, showing off a bit too much of her breasts that seem to be spilling out of the bra underneath. Her face is beautiful, pale skin with green eyes and luscious curly hair that has been pulled into a bun. Bright red lips accentuate perfectly straight, white teeth and high cheekbones fit for a magazine cover. With the exception of her somewhat unprofessional attire, she is quite beautiful. "The deli down the street has the best food, not to be confused with the one around the corner. They're trash and I've gotten food poisoning there, *twice*. You would think that the first time I would have learned my lesson." She shakes her head and stifles a chuckle. "I didn't." *Definitely wasn't expecting that.* "The copy room on the third floor has the fastest copier in the whole building. Not everyone knows it though, so don't spread it around." She holds up a third finger. "I like my coffee...black." She gives me a small smile, that I don't exactly reciprocate because I take orders from my father or one of the partners, not a glorified assistant or whatever it is she really does. "It was worth a shot." She shrugs. "Oh, and probably most importantly, because there has been quite the revolving door of women in and out of this office...don't get mixed up with Landon West. You seem like a sweet girl, Mitchell, and he'll just break your heart."

Bingo. At least she had the decency to masquerade her real intentions under lunch recommendations and her Starbucks order.

I move into my father's office to wait, as I assume he and Landon are still having it out down the hall. I set my bag down and smile as I look around the room that my mother and I helped design. My father has a corner office, and the floor to ceiling windows line two walls, giving the most gorgeous view of the New Haven skyline, and most importantly the beauty of Yale's campus. A state of the art massive desk sits in front of the windows, as well as an ungodly expensive caramel leather chair that my mother and I had to force him to get. A leather couch of the same color and quality sits against the opposite wall, and I plop down on it to wait for him to arrive. From my seat, I can see the top of the Yale cathedral, a building with such stunning architecture that it almost convinced me to enroll.

My mind drifts back to the past three years of college, and I wonder how different it would have been had I gone to Yale, or perhaps lived on campus and not at home. I'm going into my senior year at the University of Connecticut and I'm more than excited to be finished with undergrad given that it seems that the undergraduate population has two things on their mind: partying and sex.

It's gotten old.

My thoughts are interrupted by my father entering the room, his mood full of agitation, which was unusual. My father is rarely ever in a bad mood.

Preston Mitchell is tall, an attribute that completely skipped over my sister, Skyler, and me. Though I'm taller than her, I'm nowhere near the height of my father. Glasses that almost match mine sit perched on his straight nose and his curly, dirty-blonde hair—that has made more than a few people jokingly question if Skyler and I are really his children—is perfectly styled. A three-piece Armani suit makes him look like a model and, as I remember Landon's similar style, I wonder if it's a requirement for all lawyers here to look like they just stepped off the runway.

"I am so damn late." I watch as he moves across the room and slams his finger on the phone, pressing a button. "Olivia, tell me you're finished with that memo?"

"I just hit print, sir." Her voice floods the room and I'm reminded of her warning to keep away from Landon.

"Perfect, I'll be over there in two minutes." He lets the button go and grabs a few things. "Sweetheart, I am so sorry about this morning. I feel terrible that I didn't even go over anything with you yet. And that you had to hear that." He shakes his head, and it's times like this that I wonder if my father thinks I'm made of glass. Like I've never heard a swear word before. He wouldn't think twice about it if I were Skyler. But he always has gotten along with her better.

"Dad, it's fine. Can I go with you to court?"

"Not this time, Rena. Next time, I promise. This one is a closed hearing." He presses a chaste kiss to my forehead. "You'll be okay for a few hours? I'll have Olivia and my assistant Valerie check in on you, alright?"

I feel the familiar tinge of disappointment as I realize that I won't get to see a case up close and personal today. I smile, an attempt to hide my feelings, "Of course, I'll be fine." *Good thing I brought my laptop. I have a paper due next week that could use ten or so more sources.*

He's gone without another word.

An hour later, there's a knock on my father's office door and while I expect it to be Valerie, who'd already come to see me twice to see if I was hungry, thirsty, and hungry *again,* I was shocked to see the source behind the knock was none other than Landon West.

"Your dad still in court?" he asks as he slips inside like he owns the room. His voice is low and steady and, for some strange reason, I feel my heart begin to accelerate. I'm sitting at my father's desk behind my laptop, having grown tired of studying, and was currently researching Pinterest recipes to improve my eggplant parmesan. I quickly close my laptop and his lips turn upward slightly, a dimple popping out in full force. "You look guilty. Just what were you looking at?" He crosses the room and stands in front of my father's desk, his hands crossed over his broad chest.

My cheeks flush red at having been caught fooling around on the company Wi-Fi. *Could they see?* My eyes flit from left to right and then to the ceiling in an attempt to spy a camera. "Homework."

"I call BS. Pornography or illicit materials of any kind is prohibited on the firm's servers, you know." He lifts an eyebrow at me and sets his hands on the desk as he leans forward.

"I... I know. I mean I wasn't..." I stammer. I bite my bottom lip and watch as dark eyes—that I can't quite tell are brown or dark blue...or gray—drop to my mouth and darken to almost black. I feel like I'm having trouble breathing and I wonder if he can hear that my heart is about to pound out of my chest.

In a flash, the look in his eyes I've never seen before is gone and he takes a step back from his desk, probably remembering that I'm his partner's daughter and talking to me about...*pornography*...is not appropriate.

I'd never even seen pornography, I wouldn't even know where to look. *Like...porn.com?*

"I came in to check on you. Your father said you haven't eaten. So, come."

"I'm not—"

"Hungry, yes, so Valerie told me. But you need to eat something and so do I." He gives me a pointed glare that says I shouldn't argue anymore. *I ignore it.*

"Don't you have an assistant that will go fetch that for you?"

"While yes, I do, sometimes I like to get out of the building. Fresh air and all that. Come on, we'll go to this deli around the corner."

I halt in my tracks, my brain remembering that I'd heard something about that particular place. "Olivia said she got food poisoning from there." He stands at the entrance to my father's office, his hand hovering on the handle before he drops it and turns to me, effectively blocking my exit.

"You've been talking to Olivia?" he asks. *Maybe I shouldn't have said that. But, I mean, why would that concern him? She is my father's paralegal. Of course we've spoken. Maybe they really are dating?*

Not your business, Serena.

"She just offered me some advice. I guess as apart of newbie orientation." I shrug it off as if to insinuate that she hadn't told me anything important. *Like the fact that you've left a slew of broken hearts in your wake, despite the fact that you're married.*

"Really? What else did she tell you?"

"Ummm, just stuff about the fast copiers, and little things about the office *atmosphere*." I'm close enough to him to smell his cologne. It's spicy and woody and I wish I could rub up against him so that I could smell him on my skin for the rest of the day.

He eyes me, probably wondering if I'm keeping something from him. He narrows his eyes, letting me know that he doesn't buy what I'm selling. *Lawyers. They can spot a lie a mile away.* "Uh-huh. Well, you know what they say, Serena." He runs a hand through his dark-brown, wavy hair. "You can't believe everything you hear."

Three

Landon

IGNORE THE LOOKS OF HALF THE PEOPLE IN THE OFFICE. *Correction, half of the women in the office* who are more than likely seething that I'm not taking them to lunch—*or having them for lunch.*

But part of the reason I'm able to ignore them is because I'm transfixed by the woman walking a few steps in front of me. The way she swings her hips, the way her hair flows behind her, the way her slacks hug her perfectly round ass. *Fuck.* I turn my eyes away from her ass, not because I don't want to look at it, but I don't need the entirety of the office to see me ogling my partner's daughter.

I don't need to be ogling my partner's daughter period.

I shoot a look at the people whose wandering eyes need to be back on their own business and not worried about what the fuck I'm doing. They shift, nervous under my hardened gaze, as we approach the elevator. Serena, who seems to also have noticed the attention we've attracted begins to fidget as we wait for the elevator. I watch as she nervously tries to avoid my eyes as I bore a hole into the side of her head. "Don't worry about them," I tell her.

Her eyes flash to mine in shock as we move into the

elevator. "Everyone was staring," she says as the elevator doors close and we begin to descend to the lobby. Her body visibly relaxes, no longer under scrutiny of the entire tenth floor.

"That tends to happen when I walk into a room." It's the truth. My reputation, virility, and power precede me and people either drop to their knees in fear or in lust when they see me coming. One way or the other, I cause some sort of a physiological reaction in most people. I take a moment to study her beautiful features and try to ignore the stirring in my pants when she tucks a hair behind her ear and pushes her glasses further up her nose.

Fuck. Since when did that become a turn-on?

"That must get old." Her words feel like a bucket of ice water on my libido and successfully calms my erection. *It doesn't get old. I feed on that power.* "What do you mean?" I don't mean for it to sound accusatory, but the way she blinks up at me and shakes her head, I can already see her backpedaling.

Fuck that.

The doors open and I block the exit, pinning her to her spot with my gaze and I notice her gulp in response. "I just mean...it must be hard to tell when someone likes you... for you, and not just because you're this *untouchable*. People treat you like you're a God and Gods are not meant to walk amongst mortals." She ducks under my arm and walks towards the exit, her heels clicking against the marble tile with every step towards the door. I jog after her, once I've successfully closed my mouth and allowed my brain to register everything she just said.

Most importantly, her referring to me as a God.

"And just what makes you so knowledgeable on how people see me in the office?"

"I've got eyes." She shrugs. "And ears."

"What did I tell you about not believing everything you hear?" I huff, knowing that Olivia has already been filling her head with thoughts about me. *Preston is going to have to get rid of this one, and I am never going to hear the end of it.* It irritates me for a reason I can't quite pinpoint why it bothers me that Serena is listening to whatever gossip is floating around our office. I'm no stranger to the rumors. You can't sleep with half the paralegals at the firm without *someone* opening their mouth. I didn't care.

But, for some reason, I do now.

The wind whips around us, and she pulls her jacket tighter around her. It's September, which means the temperatures are dropping by the day in preparation for fall, and this is one of those cooler Indian summer days. "Let's grab a bite. I'm hungry, and I'm interested to know more about you."

Ten minutes into lunch and I feel like my dick is seconds from breaking through the zipper of my pants. I've barely touched my sandwich as I've been too focused on her mouth and the way it wraps around her fork every time she takes a bite of her salad. The way her pink lips suck on that straw in such a way I can't help but picture her lips wrapped around my dick. It takes everything in me not to reach forward and pluck the straw from her lips and warn her to cut that shit out. She eyes me curiously, but a part of me wonders if she's feigning innocence because I see a hint of playfulness in her eyes. I take a sip of the ice water in front of me wishing I could submerge my dick in it before clearing my throat.

I've got to get my shit under control. This is Preston's daughter. His twenty-one year old daughter.

And you're forty-three, not dead, my other head, the one a few feet south, replies.

Preston is a few years older than me, but not enough that he wouldn't do bodily harm to me for looking at his eldest daughter in a way I definitely shouldn't be.

"So, how's...school?" *School.* College. She hasn't even gone to law school yet. She hasn't taken the Bar. I might like a young wild girl whose limits I could test, but Serena is *too* young. Too innocent. Too naive.

"Good." She clears her throat and nods. "I'm graduating next semester." She beams with pride. "I only have five credits left to take."

"Five? Wow, you're really ahead of schedule..." It's been a while since I was in undergrad, but I could have sworn you took somewhere around fifteen per semester.

"I worked through summers and took classes during the winter session. I could have graduated this semester, but I wanted this internship. It's going to look great on my resume."

"It really will. You'll be able to get into any law school in the country with a recommendation from our firm and of course, with your last name."

She furrows her brows. "You don't think I could get in without my father's help?"

Fuck. Not what I meant. I mean...it is what I meant. To be frank, the smartest, sharpest lawyers in the world still need help getting their foot in the door. In this game, it's all about who *you know and sometimes who you've screwed.* "That's not what I—"

"Because I absolutely can."

"I don't doubt that, Serena. Knowing the right people helps, though."

"And you're one of those *right* people?"

"Your father certainly is."

She tries to hide the hurt on her face but fails miserably, and I wonder what that's about. Most future lawyers would kill to have Preston Mitchell for a father.

We sit in silence for a few moments, and just as I go to change the subject I feel the chill in the air that could only be brought about by the ice queen. The Wicked Witch of New Haven that is nine times out of ten the cause for my loss of appetite or the need for hard liquor. *What the hell is she doing here?* Jana West struts through the small deli like she owns it. Sunglasses still sitting on her face, and her shiny blonde bob chopped right under her angular chin. Her lips are painted her signature red—a red that used to make me painfully hard, but now has the power to make me flaccid within seconds. Dressed to the nines as always, she stops at our table, not even bothering to acknowledge Serena's presence.

"I went by your office. Your secretary said you came here with some new girl." She finally turns to look at Serena and as she slides her sunglasses to the top of her head, shoots icy blue daggers at her. "A little young for you, don't you think?" she sneers.

"Out," I grit at her as I point her towards the door. "Serena, wait here." I use a very different voice with her; though it's still authoritative, it's softer and calmer than the tone I plan to take with Jana. We step outside and she snorts before crossing her arms in front of her.

"Really Landon? What, is she twelve?"

"It's Preston's daughter, Jana. He's in court and she hasn't eaten. Why the fuck do you care?" I start to make a jab about her being jealous, but I don't want to open that door over what she'd have to be jealous over.

"Because you're looking at her like *she's* on the menu."

"You're delusional, which I know." I look towards the

street before pinching the bridge of my nose. "What do you want?" I'm vaguely aware of the vibration against my chest indicating that my phone is ringing. Probably people wondering where the fuck I am, as I don't usually leave the office for lunch despite what I told Serena.

"I wanted to make sure you were still taking Griff on Friday and keeping him for the weekend? He has to be at community service at nine AM Saturday."

I never forgot things when it came to Griff, that was more Jana's M.O. "You couldn't have called me to tell me that?"

"You only take calls from my fucking lawyer."

"You'd think you'd get the hint," I snap.

In the beginning of the divorce, I tried my best to be cordial. Jana wanted to leave and I made no effort to stop her. We didn't have what one would call a particularly passionate marriage *after a certain point*. Jana wanted nice things and I gave them to her. And one day, when the bags and fancy trips weren't enough to keep her happy, I came home to find a note saying she wanted a divorce and that I needed to move out.

I had turned around and gone back to the office to work through the night.

I hadn't even attempted to reconcile.

I loved Jana deeply in the beginning, but my love for her crumbled under the weight of the year-long affair she'd had a few years ago. When I first learned that she'd been sleeping with our neighbor three times a week, I was irate, devastated and was soaking my liver in whiskey every night. But I wanted to work it out. I tried to ignore my insecurities and jealousy, but I couldn't shake it. I couldn't trust her. Maybe a part of me never did. Unfortunately for me, she hadn't signed a prenup and frankly the thought of a divorce while I was on the precipice of making partner sounded financially and physically exhausting.

And so, I just checked out.

Now, she's leaving me but, to be honest, I'm not all that interested in having her stay.

Griffin knows nothing of the affair, and I plan to keep it that way. I don't want to ruin his perception of his mother, whom until recently, I still respected. Jana, however, doesn't feel the same way. I was hoping for a polite and quiet divorce where she got what she wanted and I got her the fuck out of my life, but Jana is using our divorce as an excuse to drag my name through the mud to our son and anyone who would listen.

I have *always* been there for Griff. And she knows it. He is the center of my universe. I've never missed one of his football or baseball games, never missed a parent-teacher conference, and certainly never left him stranded at school because my Swedish massage ran late. I'd walked out of a deposition upon hearing about that. Nevertheless, she'd turned Griffin against me, feeding him lies about my alleged infidelity, when actually *she'd* been the one who'd been unfaithful. That was when the gloves came off.

"I'm going to be in Miami, and I don't want him home by himself. He's sixteen and after this shit with this DUI that you can't seem to make disappear…"

"He hit another car, Jana. While someone was *in* it," I grit out. It wasn't as easy as making it go away when there were witnesses and police reports and a trip to the goddamn ER. The woman was fine, and thankfully Griffin wasn't going fast enough to do much damage to her car, but the damage to *his* life had already been done. At this point, the best I can do is get it expunged from his record when he turns eighteen.

"What's the point of having a father that's an attorney? You'd think this was the one thing you could do for him." She rolls her eyes and I resist the urge to get into it with her on the sidewalk in broad daylight like I hadn't single-handedly raised him myself the last five years.

"Are you fucking serious right now, J?" I hate myself for using my nickname for her, but Freudian slip or whatever.

"Nine thirty, do not be late. My flight is at noon."

"Whatever." I shake my head. She begins to walk away towards her shiny new Audi, that she'd purchased just before she filed for divorce when she stops in her tracks and turns around.

"Oh, I faxed over my latest revisions."

My blood boils. She was already getting more than enough considering the circumstances. "The fuck, Jana, what now?"

"I want the house in the Hamptons."

"And I *already said*, you can go fuck yourself. How much clearer would you like me to put it?"

"I decorated it!"

"Fine, take all the shit inside. I'm gutting the entire place the second the ink dries. Frankly, it's tacky as hell. But I'll be damned if you own the house, my father designed for us...for *me*." I correct.

"Ugh." She scoffs. "You are so unrefined."

"And you are such an opportunist. I have to get back to the office. Don't you have a hair appointment or something to get to? Your roots are looking a little dark," I snap at her, knowing that anything referring to her looks is a sore subject.

Her mouth drops open, but her expression shifts as her eyes focus behind me. I pray that it's just an unsuspecting passerby and not Serena Mitchell. And if it is Serena, I hope that she hadn't been present for this particularly ugly show-down between me and my soon to be ex-wife.

Jana shakes her head, darting her eyes back and forth between me and whoever's behind me. "You're pathetic, Landon." She slides her sunglasses back over her eyes and then as quick as she blew into the deli she leaves, like a tornado, leaving destruction in her wake.

Serena's quiet the entire walk back to the office. So am I, as I try to let my emotions come down from dealing with Jana. Just before we step inside she stops and it causes me to halt in my tracks. She turns to face me and looks like she's at war with herself over what to say, her beautiful face displaying a range of emotions. She opens her mouth and then closes it again, worrying her bottom lip. Without thinking, I reach un-der her chin and pull it away gently. Her pupils dilate, and a dusting of a pink hue colors her cheeks. "Do...do you want to talk about it?"

"Not particularly." I stare down at her, not wanting to move, even as people enter and exit the building on both sides of us.

"You're not pathetic, Landon."

I want to tell her I know that. That she shouldn't feel the need to reassure me about something my vengeful, estranged wife said because I won't give her what she wants in our settle-ment. Her calling me pathetic is the least vindictive or hateful thing she's said to me and yet Serena is looking at me like the eight letter word somehow bruised my ego. "You're wonder-ful," she continues. And for a second, I think she regrets her choice of words. "I don't know much about the specifics, but my dad is a great judge of character. He wouldn't speak highly of you if you weren't a good person. He says you're a great dad. Maybe because you let him tag along sometimes when you do father and son stuff," she shrugs. "You know, since he was cursed with two girls."

"You're the furthest thing from a curse, Serena." And I believe that. Preston adores both Serena and her younger sister. It's evident in the way he speaks about them both.

"You know what I mean. I just…I know you said not to believe everything you hear but…everything my father has said about you? *That* I believe."

Four

Serena

THE REST OF THE WEEK SURGES INTO THE NEXT AND I FIND myself slowly getting into the swing of things.

But I am so freaking bored.

Every day, I file, I run errands, I grab coffee, I copy. I've faxed, scanned, and copied so many things, I think this room on the third floor could be my new home.

Understandably this is the life of an intern, but this just hadn't been the expectation. Per my dad's promises, I expected a more hands-on experience. I wanted to see things in action, sit in on meetings, depo hearings, just *more*. Most importantly, I wanted to see a court case up close and personal. But every day, he leaves me in his office and I do homework like I'm a child hanging out after school, waiting for my dad so I can get a ride home.

But there has been one particularly stimulating part of this job—Landon West. Maybe it's my imagination, but I swear I feel his eyes on me everywhere. We haven't had lunch since the first day, but he always checks in to make sure I've eaten before he sends out for food. His eyes seem to follow me around the room whenever we are in the same place.

We rode in the elevator alone today and with each passing

floor, I could feel something crackling between us. His gaze traced the side of my face for the duration of the ten floor ascension, his tall, lean body pressed against the wall of the elevator with his hands in his pockets. I was too afraid to even breathe, let alone look at him. As soon as we got to our floor I all but fled from the elevator without a look in his direction. After that, I felt his gaze on me for the rest of the day. He even followed me to the copy room and stared at me from across the room when I was delegated the basic task of scanning a memo.

What is he doing to me?

I'm staring at the ceiling of my bedroom going over and over that tense interaction in the elevator just as my phone begins to ring.

Heavy breathing fills my ears and for a moment I consider hanging up, thinking that the unknown number that called me in the middle of the night is some sort of prank…or the beginning of a scary movie. But then his silky voice washes over me like warm honey and I have to hold my breath to prevent myself from letting the gasp escape my lips.

"Mitchell." I blink my eyes a few times and sit further up in bed, tossing my iPad to the side. I tuck some hair behind my ear and flatten my messy bed-head with my hand as if he can *see* me.

Mr. West is on the tip of my tongue, but after our interaction today, I decide to let his name fall from my lips in a whisper. "Landon?"

The silence is deafening and my heart pounds in my chest. *The pounding is even more aggressive between my legs.* My cheeks slowly heat up and I hold my breath so he doesn't hear my ragged intakes of air. *What is happening? Is this an orgasm?* I've been turned on before but never…like *this*. I can hear his breathing, but the silence stretches on, neither of us saying anything.

"Shit." I hear him grumble and the word must have a direct line to my clit because it throbs instantly. I look around my room, trying to find something that will calm my erratic heartbeat that is pounding between my legs and my eyes find a picture on my dresser of me my mom, Skyler, and *my dad*.

Not helping.

"I called the wrong Mitchell," I hear from the other end. "I meant…" he slurs slightly and I'm starting to understand the reason for this 2 AM phone call. "I meant to call P."

"Well, you've got me," I quip. My eyes widen at the words I've let slip and the potential implication. I fiddle with my glasses as I nervously wait for his response.

"I do," he murmurs, and I wonder if it wasn't meant for me to hear.

"Where are you?"

"Bar." He grunts. "Can't find my fucking keys." I hear shuffling through the phone and faint noises in the background and a surge of jealousy courses through my veins as I think about a possible woman there.

"Well, you shouldn't be driving anyway. I would hope the bartender would have taken them from you."

"Oh. Maybe. Shit. Did you take my fucking keys?" He barks to someone. "That's a two hundred thousand dollar car, don't even think about it."

I roll my eyes. "He's trying to save your life, Landon. You shouldn't be driving. Besides, what kind of message are you teaching your son, if you do what he's in trouble for?"

He's silent and for a split second I wonder if I've gone too far. "I should take you over my knee for that."

I ignore the moisture leaking out between my legs and

wetting my panties. I rub my legs together trying to quiet the roar between them. God, how do women live like this? It's *this* intense, every time you get turned on? I lift the hem of my underwear and see the moisture glistening between my thighs. *Holy cow.* I realize I haven't said anything, so I stammer out an apology. "I…Sorry, it's none of my business."

"You're damn right it's not…But shit, if you aren't right."

I lick my lips, trying to wet the dryness in my mouth and I let out a breath. "Were you calling my dad to come get you?"

"Yeah."

"You know there's an Uber app for that."

"Ubers are for millennials and underaged kids who get drunk at bars," he slurs.

I purse my lips, as a scowl finds my face. "How else do you suggest getting home?"

"My responsible best friend who usually picks me up."

"I can come get you," I blurt out before I have the chance to think that this is *not* a good idea. I feel the line blurring, and I find myself in uncharted territory with Landon West. I saw the way he looked at me, and I can't help but look at him the same way.

Intrigue. Curiosity. Forbidden interest.

Something is happening between us and it's happening fast. At twenty-one, I've never had a boyfriend, and I've kissed exactly two boys, neither of which with my tongue and yet I find myself wanting to run mine over every inch of Landon.

Oh my God.

"I don't want you out at 2 AM by yourself, Serena." His voice is authoritative and I can almost hear the growl in his tone.

"How else are you going to get home?"

"I'll figure it out."

"That's ridiculous." I'm off the bed and pulling a sweat-shirt over my head and a pair of shorts over my bare legs. I cradle the phone between my ear and my shoulder and grab my keys. "Text me your location. I'm coming to get you." I hang up the phone without another word. While I'm waiting for his response, I rush into my bathroom and brush my teeth. I pull my hair out of the messy bun and let it fall down my back in waves before swiping some peach lip balm across my lips. Right on cue my phone chirps from the other room.

Unknown Number: Old Town Irish Pub. Do not get out of the car. Text when you're here.

I frown, wondering why I'm not allowed to get out of the car. Is he embarrassed to be seen with me? *I'm sure being picked up by a college student isn't high on his list of proud moments.* My phone pings again.

Unknown Number: I mean it, Serena.

I pull up to the bar and crane my neck towards the entrance to see if I see him. When I don't, I pull my phone out and dial his number. When he doesn't respond I text him to let him know I'm here before attempting to call him again. After ten minutes of waiting, I decide to go in against his warning. I certainly don't want to be waiting out here all night. I push through the doors of the dive bar and I'm immediately hit with the smell of booze, smoke, and a smell I don't recognize. A round of catcalls ring through the air and I feel everyone's eyes on me. To say I'm out of my element is the understatement of the century. I find myself wishing I had a can of pepper spray or at least some basic knowledge of self-defense. I swallow as I try to back out of the bar to bolt towards the safety of my car.

The establishment is dim, the wallpaper drab and dingy and in desperate need of repapering. A bar sits in the middle of the room, a pool table is set up in the corner, and a dartboard hangs on the other side. High top tables line the perimeter with bottles of cheap beer and high balls of whiskey glasses littering the surfaces. The poor lighting gives everyone a yellow-ish glow underneath the fog of cigarette smoke.

I didn't know people could still smoke indoors?

"Hey, baby. You looking for me?" I hear from behind me as I'm still backing up, and shivers run down my spine—but not in the good way. I spin around to find a man in his mid-thirties dressed in a suit, his black hair falling over his forehead and eyes so dark and sinister I panic that I've come face to face with Satan himself.

"No…" I stammer. "I…" I start to walk in the opposite direction since he's blocking the door, trying to get away from the creepy man when I walk right into a wall of muscle.

"What did I fucking tell you?" His voice is low in my ear and when I look up I'm staring at a very angry Landon West. He towers over me, his build engulfing my small frame as he wraps his arms around me and tucks me into his side. "Unless you want me to rip your eyes from your face, I suggest you move it the fuck along," he says through gritted teeth at Lucifer. His hands are firmly wrapped around me and I take a minute to press my face into his jacket.

Gosh, he smells good.

Clean and manly. Like fresh laundry and whiskey.

The other man chuckles. "Good for you, dude, what did you pluck her out of grade school?"

I groan inwardly, feeling embarrassed that the vast age gap between us has been brought up yet again, and when I look up Landon looks ready to rip his head off. Before I can suggest it's time for us to go, we're on the move out of the bar without another glance.

"Car, Serena. Before I go back there and get my ass disbarred." I point at the silver Audi, an early graduation present from my parents that is sitting a few spaces from the entrance to the bar. He all but pushes me into the car before slamming my door shut and climbing in next to me. "I told you to wait in the car."

"You weren't answering. I called and texted you. I waited for like ten minutes," I say in my defense. I don't want him to be mad at me, and I definitely don't want to get him into any trouble.

"You can't follow simple instructions? Fuck, your father would have my head if he knew you were in a place like that."

My father would have your head if he saw the way you look at me. The words are on the tip of my tongue but I swallow them down.

"I won't tell if you won't," I tell him and, in this moment, my body has started to recognize the proximity of Landon West to me. My insides start to hum as I survey the enclosed space. He is close enough for me to reach out to touch, to grab, to…I bite my lip and keep my eyes trained forward, not wanting to look at the gorgeous creature to my right.

"You're trouble, Serena."

"I think you're confusing me with the wrong Mitchell sister. I am far from trouble." I had never been a partier. However, my younger sister, Skyler, is always the life of the party, and she drags me along with her every once in a while—mostly when mom and dad demand she needs a chaperone. She's outgoing and fun and everyone wants to be around her. I, on the other hand, am the shy, introverted wallflower that would rather spend her Saturday nights inside, reading a book or cooking with Mama.

"No…" He shakes his head and scrubs a hand over his jaw and the sounds of his fingers over his scruff pierce the silence. "You're trouble…for me."

His words make my heart slam into my ribcage. I always thought that boys didn't seem to notice me much. Skyler says they notice me all the time, but I'm too uptight to pay them the time of day. *That wasn't exactly true.* They just made me nervous. I wore my feelings on my face and I could blush crimson red at the drop of a hat.

According to Skyler, I have *no chill.*

I realize I haven't started the car, but I can't bring myself to break the tension. "Don't you have a girlfriend?"

"A what now?" His eyebrows almost fly to his hairline.

I adjust my position on the soft leather as I prepare to ask the question I've been dying to know since I saw them this morning. "Olivia? Isn't she your girlfriend?"

"Oh…honey…no."

I scoff at his reaction. "Don't patronize me."

"I wasn't…I…" he huffs. "I don't owe you an explanation," he snaps, though I can tell he regrets it.

Somewhere in the distance I hear laughter, and my eyes zero in on a drunk couple stumbling by. *I wish my life were that carefree. Ever.* I turn back to Landon. "I didn't say you did, but you're breaking about a hundred rules, you know."

"I don't see how that's any of your concern. Unless of course…you're jealous."

"That's absurd, and I wouldn't insult the person who's driving you home, Mr. West." I finally find the urge to start the car, and the engine hums. *Am I jealous? Do I want to be Olivia?*

Don't be dense, Serena. Of course you do. That pesky inner voice—that often takes on the lilting tone of my younger sister, Skyler—perks up.

"Nice car."

"Thank you."

"I bet you've had some fun in it." He gives me a boyish grin and I wonder how many girls have gotten into trouble as a result of that smile.

I narrow my eyebrows wondering what his words mean. "I haven't had it very long, so I haven't done anything too crazy."

"I lost my virginity in an Audi." He chuckles. "My father's to be exact. He was pissed when he found the condom wrapper. But mostly because my mother thought it was his…" He shakes his head and I hear the hurt in his voice despite his dark humor regarding his father's infidelity.

"I certainly don't plan to lose mine in one," I blurt out. I hadn't meant to come off bitchy or superior but I worry that's exactly how I sounded; like the uptight girl who is saving herself for marriage or Prince Charming or God.

When I don't hear a response, I turn my head towards him and he's gaping at me as if he has no idea what to say. "Your father will be so proud."

Not where I thought that was going.

I blink at him. "Excuse me?"

"I mean…"

"I would appreciate if you kept my sex life, or lack thereof, out of your topics of conversation with my father."

"No father wants to hear about their child having sex. He'll be pleased to know that you're still…pure." His words sound innocent but the look in his eye and the tone of his voice is anything but.

"Can we stop this now?"

"Why are you a virgin?"

So, that's a no on ending this conversation then? "Because I am?"

"I just…how?"

"Like biologically?"

"Smart ass," he grumbles, but I see a smile playing at his lips. "You know what I mean."

"I just…I haven't met the right guy, I guess."

"Ah, Mr. Right."

"Not necessarily. I would be okay with losing it to *Mr. Right Now*, but I haven't found him either."

"I find it hard to believe *you* have trouble getting a date." I look away from the steering wheel and find his gaze which is fixed on my bare legs. I snap my eyes away from him, hoping he didn't see me.

"I'm busy. I go to school and I'm very committed to my work. I'm graduating next semester, and now I'm working at your firm. I just don't have time."

He squares his shoulders, his posture rigid, and I find myself wanting to run my hands over the sharp ridges of his body. "I happen to see the way some of the interns look at you." His voice is even but I can hear the irritation. I can *feel* his growl rattling through my bones.

"Me?" I squeak.

"Yes, particularly when you wear that navy pencil skirt of yours. Or that black dress that flares out at your hips. Really anything that shows off your legs. Seriously, do you own a fucking pair of pants?"

I shrug. "I like dresses and skirts."

"Yeah, so do half the men at our firm. It drives me fucking insane."

"You say the F-word a lot."

He throws his head back in a howl and rubs his eyes. "The F-word?"

"Yes? You know…"

"Fuck? You mean the word *fuck*, Serena?"

I gulp. I feel like the word takes on a whole new meaning when Landon says it. It's not a dirty, bad word. It's a dirty, delicious word that I want to scream as he does bad things to me. "Yes."

"Do you not swear?"

"I was taught that ladies don't swear." *Though I slip up from time to time, especially when I'm arguing with Skyler.* He chuckles and nods, but I can see he wants to say something. "What, West?"

"Ladies that *don't* swear, haven't been thoroughly fucked."

Five

Serena

FOR THE FIRST FEW MINUTES OF THE DRIVE, WE ARE QUIET. The only sounds are the constant hum of my car. I sense movement in my peripheral and when I sneak a peek at Landon I notice him regarding me, his index finger resting on his lip. I try to ignore the sensation below that became amplified the second he talked about what could potentially have me swearing like a sailor.

"So, why UConn?" He breaks the silence.

"What do you mean?" I've been asked this question a hundred times, mostly with genuine curiosity. With my grades and SAT scores, everyone has an opinion about why I chose a state school for college.

"A smart girl like you...didn't want to go Ivy? Your father has been bragging about you for years. I know you had your pick of schools." *Bragging about me? Surely, he meant Skyler...*

"I wanted to stay close to home."

He snorts. "What about Yale?"

"UConn offered more money. I got into Yale, but they didn't offer to pay."

I didn't see it, but I know he rolled his eyes. "Your parents can afford it."

Goosebumps pop up on my skin and tears prickle in my eyes as the sense of vulnerability washes over me. I'd never told anyone the truth, never spoken the words aloud.

I clear my throat and focus my eyes on the road.

"So, there's a story."

"I just…I'm used to being the smartest person in the room."

"Big fish in a small pond. I get it," he adds.

"And if I went to a school like Yale…"

He nods in understanding. "I see. You were scared."

"I wasn't scared. I just…wasn't ready for all the other big fish."

"So…scared."

"Do you want me to leave you on the side of the road?" I point a finger out the window towards the rows of trees we are passing as I move down the two-lane highway. He doesn't say anything for a moment, so I continue. "I'll go to Yale for law school, happy?"

"No," he says immediately. "You need to go away for law school. Somewhere that requires you to move out of your parents' guest house. You need to experience life away from Mom and Dad. Have you ever been anywhere without them?"

"I've been to Italy."

"Did you stay with family?"

I feel a flare of jealousy as I think about how different Skyler's and my experiences were when we visited the motherland. Aside from the Italian boy that broke her heart, she had the time of her life exploring the city and immersing herself in the culture by living it. I spent most of my time there in the kitchen with my aunt, watching Italian telenovelas and *reading* about the culture.

"I've been to Greece," I add. "Without family."

"Better. Who did you go with?"

I take a breath, knowing he'll have something smart to say about my answer. "A youth group."

"So, church. Damn what kind of youth group goes to Greece? I thought churches went to third world countries and built houses and taught orphaned children. Since when do they go to Mykonos or Santorini?"

"Don't be like that. It was a team building experience before we went to high school."

He raises an eyebrow at me. "Sure, Bambi. Look, you're twenty-one, you can't hide out in your parents' guest house forever. This is the time of your life. Have you even tasted alcohol?"

I'm confused by his nickname. *A baby deer? Was that a term of endearment? Or an insult?* "Bambi? What does that mean?"

"Answer my question first."

"Yes, of course I have. And I've even been drunk a few times."

"Whoa there, rebel without a cause." He puts his hands out as if he's bracing himself.

"Shut up." I giggle and my heart skips a beat for a second. *Did I just say that to an adult? Like a real adult?*

"You should see your face. As much as you probably deserve a spanking for that, I'll let it slide because your expression is priceless. Take the next exit." He points, like he hadn't just talked about spanking me.

"That's the second time you've said that...about spanking me."

"Intrigued, are we?"

"No...I just. No one has ever...I've never been..."

"No, Preston and Viv probably never laid a hand on you or Littlest Mitchell, did they? Their perfect princesses."

"What reason would I need to be spanked? As you've pointed out more than once tonight, I'm pretty well-behaved and boring." I try my best to hide the hurt in my voice.

"You aren't boring. I would never call you boring. Naive. Inexperienced, maybe. But not boring. When I called you Bambi, I just meant you were doe-eyed. Those beautiful eyes of yours are so large and innocent and full of wonder. It's refreshing to meet someone who hasn't had their humanity completely ripped from them. Who's not jaded and angry. Someone who believes good still exists."

"There's still a lot of good out there, Landon."

"There's a lot of bad too, Serena. I hope you never see it. But unfortunately, it's a part of life."

"You're so cynical."

He doesn't respond. I pull into a neighborhood and I frown as I see the size of the homes. They're not small, but they're smaller than the home I knew he lived in before. "You live here?"

"I moved out when Jana filed and…" he clears his throat, "a lot of money is tied up in the proceedings. She doesn't have a prayer at getting half, but my financial advisor thought I should have something understated, and I didn't need much. Third on the right." He points and I pull into the driveway and put the car in park. "Thank you for the ride, Mitchell."

I nod and my teeth find their way onto my bottom lip as I resist the urge to say what I've been thinking all night. "You know, I'm beginning to think you called me on purpose. You don't seem all that drunk."

"When you get to be my age, you learn how to keep it together. You're reckless in different ways. Maybe I can walk a straight line or hold a coherent conversation, but I also make dangerous decisions. Let alcohol convince me to touch things I shouldn't. *Want* things I shouldn't."

I let out a breath slowly as I let his words sink in.

I want him to touch me.

To want me.

I find myself wondering what the inside of his home looks like. Where he sleeps, eats, showers…but I know going into his house is the equivalent of Alice stumbling down that famous rabbit hole.

Am I ready for that?

"Umm do you need help, or…anything? I mean, should I come in or?" I stop, when I see the look he's giving me.

Something dark flashes across his features and it calls out to something inside of me. "You don't know what you're asking. Don't tempt the lion, Bambi."

"I just thought…"

"Thought what? I would touch my best friend's virgin daughter?" The way he says it, it doesn't sound like it's something he *couldn't* see himself doing. The thought sends goosebumps all over my skin.

"No…I—"

"Kiss her, fuck her, make her come harder than she's ever dreamed of? You've never come before, have you, Bambi?" His voice is low and hoarse and I wonder if it's the alcohol making him sound that way or something else.

His words make me squirm in my seat, but I try not to let on that I'm thoroughly embarrassed. "That's not your business."

"Tell me. Do you touch yourself? Rub a finger over your clit? You've never been penetrated so I know you won't think that feels good, but have you discovered that button that can make you quiver with desire?"

I'm grateful for the darkness, the only lights illuminated are on my dashboard, but when I look over, his features are as clear as day.

"Are you trying to embarrass me?" I squeak. No one has ever spoken to me like that. It makes my heart race, the space between my legs pound harder, and I feel myself getting short of breath.

"No. I'm trying to empower you. Ask for what you want, Serena."

"I— I don't know what I want."

"Sure, you do. Ask me, Bambi."

"You'll laugh at me."

"No, I won't." His fingers reach up and tuck a lock of hair behind my ear. I look over at him and when my tongue darts out to wet my lips, he groans. "Fuck. You're so beautiful. It actually hurts to look at you."

"Why?"

"You know why, Serena. It would ruin years of friendship."

"I wouldn't…tell…" I choke out, as I step closer to the proverbial rabbit hole. I peek down the hole and I don't see anything, just black.

What's down there anyway?

Probably an orgasm! My inner Skyler perks up.

"Tell me to get out of the car, Serena," he says. I know it's not what he wants but I hear the implication in his hoarse voice. *Here's your out. Take it.*

I don't.

"What do you want, Serena?"

The car is silent as he prepares for my answer. *Say it, Serena. Like he said, ask for what you want.* "I'm twenty-one and…I've never been…properly kissed."

"Everything about you is *proper*, Serena. Be more specific for me."

"I've never made out with anyone." My cheeks flame. *Do adults say make-out?*

"Is that all you want?" I don't respond because I don't know if I'm prepared to go further.

"I have to crawl before I walk."

"Fair."

"And that's even saying you'd be willing to…teach me to walk." I look up at him as sexy as I can, but I feel like I'm failing with my glasses in the way. Yet, the growl that escapes his throat makes me believe I succeeded.

"When you look at me like that, I'm likely to give you anything you want."

"Maybe just the kiss…for now." I nibble on my bottom lip, and his pupils dilate as they fix on my mouth.

He leans forward across my console so that we are practically nose to nose. I fiddle with the legs of my glasses prepared to take them off when he speaks. "Leave them."

"It's not hard to kiss with them?"

"No. Leave it," he demands. "One day, I'll kiss you somewhere else and make you watch me behind those sexy glasses of yours."

"Where?" I had a guess, but I wanted to hear him say it.

He leans back slowly and I can tell he's studying me to see if I really don't know, or if I'm just messing with him. "You know where." He pauses. "If that's something you're interested in." He winks.

I swallow, my body unprepared for the way his words make it feel. I feel too hot, and before I can remind myself that I'm not wearing a bra underneath my tank top, I've pulled my sweatshirt off. "Holy fuck, Serena, goddamn." I look down and see my hardened nipples poking through the thin cotton.

"Oh. I…I was just hot."

"Yes, you fucking are. Come here, Bambi." I'm sure

where *here* is, but before I can question it, he's pulled me across the console into his lap. "I'm crossing all the fucking lines right now but you're just so perfect. You're so untouched and pure and *fuck*. I would ruin you, Serena."

I gulp. "Do I want that?"

"You're asking?" His fingers ghost over the swell of my breast, stroking the skin but not going lower. My breath hitches feeling his touch somewhere so intimate even if it's not my nipples.

I nod. "I'm curious."

His hands find my face and he cradles it like I'm the most precious thing. "Be careful what you ask for, Serena."

"You'll...touch me?" I squeak. I wonder if his touch would quiet the roar between my legs. If his kiss would lick away the tingle. I move slightly in his lap, my body moving on its own, to seek some type of relief.

He groans and I feel *it* hardening beneath me. "You're killing me, Serena."

"Sorry." I bite my bottom lip, unsure, as he moves closer.

"My little baby deer. Don't be nervous." His lips find the base of my throat before floating up my neck, leaving kisses in his wake. He nibbles on my chin, his tongue darting out to lick the skin.

"Okay," I whisper as his lips ghost over mine. He nibbles on my bottom lip, sucking the skin into his mouth before letting it go with a pop. His hand moves to grip the back of my neck and then his tongue is probing my mouth for entrance. His tongue tastes like whiskey and a hint of mint and I almost melt in his arms. *Oh my God, my first real kiss.* My hands find his face as we find a rhythm that has him groaning into my mouth. His tongue is wild and aggressive at times and slow and languid at others. I just follow his lead and let him control

43

the motions. I hadn't kissed anyone else like this, but something told me he was by far one of the best.

I never want this to end.

I feel my nipples hardening under my shirt to the point of pain and I'm suddenly anxious for his touch. I begin to rock against him, desperate for some relief when he grips my hips, halting my movements.

"Serena," he tightens his grip as he holds me in place, "stop being a tease," he commands.

"I'm not," I retort.

"Maybe not on purpose, but you rubbing against my dick is not helping me stay in control."

My heart slams against my chest at his confession. "Maybe I want you *out* of control."

"Getting out of control will end with my dick fucking all three of your holes, now relax."

I pull back from his lips which had found its way back to my neck. "All...three?" I cock my head to the side.

He raises an eyebrow and my eyes widen and my lips form an O shape. I clench without thinking. "You're not putting anything there."

"We'll see."

"Yeah, we will," I quip.

"Don't talk back to me, Serena."

I frown. "You're not in control here, Landon."

"Oh, you think?" He grips my jaw. "The second I touch you, I mean *really* touch you, you'll be begging for my dick. *Everywhere.*"

I let out a breath before I lean in and brush my lips over his gently. I close my eyes and lose myself in his kiss once more, as the feeling of free falling into the unknown overtakes me.

Six

Landon

THE KNOCK ON THE DOOR OF MY OFFICE ALMOST SENDS MY coffee flying across the room when I jump to my feet. I've been tense since I woke up this morning. I'd jacked off twice to the carnal images of feeling up my friend's daughter in her car with my tongue down her throat, but nothing was dulling the ache. Nothing was quieting the roar in my cock. The crazy part is I don't regret it. I don't regret one second of the compromising position Serena Mitchell and I were in as we sat in my driveway last night. But that's not why I'm tense. I'm tense because I want it again.

And again.

She's like a drug; I had my first taste last night, and now I'm craving another hit. My hands keep flexing on their own as they remember cupping her perfect ass as she sat in my lap. My cock hardens every time I remember her rubbing against my dick. My mouth waters every time I remember running my tongue along her neck. I want my mouth on hers. Need her taste on my tongue. Need my hands wrapped around her tiny frame as she rubs against me.

Fuck.

My cock has already decided that Serena is on the other

side of the door but it deflates instantly when I open the door and I'm met with Olivia, a cheeky smile plastered on her face before she sashays past me like she has the right to. I leave the door open so she's not confused as to what's going to happen here. She's wearing that green pencil skirt that brings out the color in her eyes, that just last week, I had hiked around her waist as I feasted on her cunt.

"Miss Barrett?"

"Landon," she purrs—actually purrs—at me. I hate when women do it so obviously. That forcibly sexy voice women take on when it's not necessary. When men want you, they want you. The throaty voice, the hair flip, the sexy eyes—it's not necessary once a man's dick has been in your mouth. We don't need the seduction at that point.

We're a sure thing.

Unless we're not interested.

And I'm no longer interested.

"Can I help you with something?" I stand in front of the open door, hoping she gets the picture that no one is getting off in this room.

Well, maybe me and Serena...

"I thought I could help *you*." She smirks.

"Miss Barrett, you told me our arrangement was over." I use my most professional voice, not loud enough for anyone outside of my office to hear, but it still creates the illusion that we are maintaining some level of professionalism.

"I think...I was hasty in my decision..." She looks behind me towards the open door. "Can we close the door?"

"Nope, we can't. I have court soon, and I need to do a few things before then."

"Like Mr. Mitchell's daughter?" she asks, her voice laced with judgment.

I don't ignore the spike in my adrenaline *or my cock* as I think about the "new girl" in question. "Watch yourself, Olivia."

She shakes her head and rolls her eyes as she looks around my room. "You are such a cliché, Landon. The forbidden fruit really does it for you, huh? It's not enough that she's an *intern*," she says with disdain, like the position is beneath her, like *she* didn't start off as one herself.

"She's already off limits, but you've got to take it a step further. Your partner's daughter who's young enough to be *your* daughter. What, is she a few years older than your son?" She scrunches her nose in disgust and tosses her hair over her shoulder. "I guess you do love a girl with daddy issues."

"Enough, Olivia," I snarl, my voice low, and even as I remember the open door behind me, I take a step towards her. "You wanted out. So, you're out. You also said you were going to claim I sexually harassed you and forced you into a sexual relationship, so excuse me for not being eager to trust you again. To *fuck* you again." I take a step closer to her and she backs up. "This conniving little ploy to get me to touch you due to some misplaced jealousy you have over Serena Mitchell is ridiculous. You said I wasn't good for you, Olivia, so move on, and leave Serena out of it."

Her mouth drops open and I can see she's not like the others. The others cried, some even begged, some asked for one final fuck that I was more than happy to oblige, but most of them had their notice sent to HR seconds after their orgasms had waned. Olivia is different. Olivia has spunk and fire and a take no shit attitude that will make her the perfect partner one day. Sure, she has her share of issues that stem from a neglectful father, but she'll make one hell of a lawyer. It's part of the reason I was drawn to her.

She shakes her head with a wicked gleam in her eye. "You should leave Serena alone, Landon. She's so young and naive, you'll just ruin her like all the others…Haven't you broken enough hearts?" She doesn't give me a chance to respond before she's out the door. I resist the urge to call her back and chew her out when I'm reminded of the conversation I had with P just last week.

"I swear on all that's holy, West, if you cause another one of my paralegals to quit…Keep it the fuck in your pants, for God's sake. What's the matter with you? Do you know how hard it is to find a paralegal to keep up with me? How hard it is to break one in and train them to my exact preferences? I can't keep finding a new one every six weeks. Fuck someone in another department. Fuck Frank's team, I don't care. Just stay away from mine."

I close the door harder than I intended and spend the rest of the morning in my office, letting Olivia and Preston's words that I do more harm than good swirl around my brain.

When I finally emerge from my office, my body is on high alert wondering just when I'm going to run into the sweet, young woman that I'd had in my arms just last night. Long gone are the self-deprecating thoughts I'd had in response to Olivia's words. Now, I want to find Serena. A woman who is like no one I'd ever met let alone kissed. My eyes are all over the office, looking for her, and for a brief moment I think about going to Preston's office to see where I can find her.

No, that's too obvious. The less Preston knows about our interactions the better.

A gaggle of interns whisk past me, giggling into their coffees and shooting me nervous glances from over their files. I let out a breath, suddenly needing another cup of coffee but instead of sending Valerie out, I opt for the break room.

As soon as I turn the corner, a familiar scent surrounds me. It isn't something I would necessarily call sweet. It's spicy and the sense of nostalgia hits my brain before I can put the pieces together.

And then I see her.

She's standing with her back to me as she waits for her coffee at the Keurig. Her hair is pulled into a high sleek ponytail and even from behind I see her fiddling with her glasses. She's wearing a gray high waisted pencil skirt with a white cap-sleeved shirt tucked into it. Sheer stockings adorn her legs that I want to pull off with my teeth as I discover if they're full stockings or the sexy ones that stop mid-thigh. As I ogle her from behind, I expect her to feel my gaze. To sense my presence. To know I'm behind her, salivating. But she doesn't move.

Can't she feel the heat between us? Am I the only one that notices this stifling tension?

"Serena." The word is out of my mouth like a command. Like that word alone is enough to tell her what I want. Her shoulders square and her back stiffens as she turns around and gives me a weak smile.

"Hi, Landon." Her words are so quiet, like a whisper, and for a moment I wonder if she's nervous, if her heart is pounding in her chest. Her lips quirk up in a smile and her eyes light up behind her glasses. "Do you want some coffee?"

Coffee? She thinks I want to talk about coffee?

"No. I mean…yes. But…" I cross the room, grateful that there's no one in here. "Where's your father?"

"Court."

"He didn't take you…again?" I ask. *What is the point of having her intern here if she isn't going to get to see anything?*

"It's another closed hearing."

"Bullshit." I grunt. *We take interns with us all the time.* Her face falls and I wonder if I've confirmed what she'd been thinking. "What are you doing this afternoon?" I ask, wanting nothing more than to take that sad look off her face, and knowing exactly how to do it.

"Ummm…" she starts.

"You're coming with me."

"With you…?" She cocks her head to the side in question, and I'm reminded that perhaps she thinks I mean something else.

"To court," I finish.

"Really?" Her eyes widen even brighter than when she saw me for the first time just moments ago, and for a moment, my ego is bruised.

*She's more excited at the idea of going to court, than the idea of going to court with…*me.

I straighten my tie slightly and take a step back, forcing my hands into my pockets so that I don't touch her. "Yes, I go in at two. You're welcome to come."

"I would love to, thank you!" She claps her hands and spins around to grab the coffee behind her. "Here," she says. "I was making it for you anyway. I…I asked Valerie what you liked." I expect a blush or any sign of nervousness but her features give nothing away.

"Thank you." No one had ever made me coffee without me asking. Correction: telling. Jana didn't even make me coffee in the morning when we were married.

She rarely made me anything for that matter.

She hands me the cup and when our fingers graze each other, a spark ignites from her fingertips, setting me on fire. The room is so quiet I hear her breath hitch and that sound is enough to make me broach the subject.

I rub the back of my neck. "Serena…" I start when I'm suddenly aware that we are no longer alone.

"Hey, Serena." The voice is of the male persuasion. Young, with a deep timbre that triggers my possessiveness. I am the jealous type through and through, which is why things with Jana could have never worked out once I learned of her infidelity. So, anyone sniffing around Serena when just yesterday I'd kissed those perfect lips with every intention to kiss her everywhere else, is not. fucking. happening.

Her eyes flit to mine like she can hear every thought in my head. Her beautiful hazel eyes are nervous and wondering if I'm going to tell this guy, whose name I probably don't even know to back the fuck off. I turn towards the source of the voice and sure enough, no clue. *Jake? Jack? James? No idea, he's a mid-level associate, I think, but I can't be sure.*

"Hey, Justin," she says with a friendly smile.

He must finally notice that they're not alone because he acknowledges me with a nod, assumedly trying to impress Serena, because most mid-level associates are scared to death of me. They go to Preston most of the time, or Frank if it's something basic and easy. "Mr. West."

I nod back. For a moment the three of us stand there in the awkward silence as both he and I wait for the other guy to make their exit. "Serena, are we still on for lunch, today?" he finally speaks, when he realizes I'm not going anywhere.

She looks at me for a beat, before finding his gaze. "Yes." She nods. "I mean, sure. That sounds good." Her tone is non-committal but her words are enough to awaken the beast.

Fuck that.

"Actually, Miss Mitchell will be joining me in court this afternoon." I turn to Serena. "Unless you've changed your mind about coming?" The wording I choose doesn't escape me and most women I know would pick up on the innuendo instantly, *but not Serena.*

"Oh, no...n...no." She shakes her head before turning to Justin. "Justin, I'm so sorry. Let's raincheck lunch, though?"

Yeah, okay. We'll see about that.

I half expect him to combat her excuse by inviting her to join *him* in court, in which case I would have to get whatever bullshit hearing he has moved to another day, or have him removed from said case altogether. *And that would be a fuck ton of paperwork.* I'm grateful when he nods and makes his exit with a promise that they would rain check tomorrow.

Think again.

My eyes snap to hers as soon as we are alone. "Don't have lunch with him."

Her timid gaze meets mine and her lips part slightly. "What?"

"Lunch. With him. Or any other man. No lunches, no dinners, no coffees. None of that shit."

"Why?"

Is she fucking with me? "What do you mean, why?" I'm used to women understanding that I'm a jealous caveman. That I don't want other guys getting the wrong idea about a woman that belongs to *me.*

"It's a simple question." She shrugs. "I don't have anyone else to have lunch with. Why can't I have lunch with him?" She blinks her eyes a few times and every time her thick lashes fan out over her flawless skin my cock swells in my pants.

"Because I said so, Serena." *Smooth, West. What are we kids? Might as well tell everyone on the floor, that Serena is your toy to play with and no one else can touch her.*

"Are you...jealous?"

"Yes."

"Oh." Her eyes widen like she wasn't expecting me to say that. "I don't like him, though. You shouldn't be jealous."

Holy fuck is she naive. I am so out of my league here. "Not the point. I don't want him getting the wrong idea."

"Which is what?"

I huff, growing irritated with this conversation. "That you're available."

"I am available."

"The hell you are," I snap. I take a step closer to her, but she holds her ground, not taking a step back even as I invade her personal space. "Do you remember last night?"

She nods her head, her eyes wide, unblinking and innocent as her ponytail bobs up and down. "I wasn't sure *you* did."

"As you pointed out, I wasn't all that drunk."

"Did you call me on purpose?"

I shake my head. "No. That really was an accident."

She doesn't say anything for a few minutes, her eyes studying me and for some reason, it makes me nervous, so I take a step back. I'm not used to women staring me square in the eye. I'm used to them averting their gaze. I'm used to our eye contact being on my terms, when I command them to look at me. "Okay fine, no meals with other men. Does that mean you'll do the same?"

"The same what?"

"No meals with other women? No Olivia?" She raises an eyebrow at me and it makes me wonder just what Olivia has disclosed to her.

"My relationship with Olivia is over," I tell her honestly.

"But there was a relationship."

I clear my throat. I don't want to get into the logistics about Olivia or any other women. "An arrangement."

"Is that what you want with me? An *arrangement*?"

"You ask a lot of questions."

"I want a lot of answers," she quips and the words leaving her mouth turn me on almost as much as her mouth itself.

"I'm not capable of…much, Serena." Sex. *Very good sex.* Buying you whatever you want. A weekend in the Hamptons. That is the extent of what I can offer a woman. I'm in the middle of a tumultuous divorce and a rift with my son that I'm desperate to fix. I don't have an excess of time that I can commit to a woman who doesn't get it.

"People are capable of anything…if they want it bad enough." She raises an eyebrow at me.

"You'll make one hell of a lawyer one day, Mitchell." I nod at her.

"That doesn't exactly answer my question but…I'll let it slide for now." She takes a deep breath and lets it out slowly before she speaks again. "You scare me. This…" she points back and forth between us, "scares me. I barely slept a wink after I left your house last night. And maybe I'm not supposed to tell you that. Maybe I'm supposed to play it cool and act like it wasn't a big deal for me. But because I'm twenty-one and I have zero experience with the opposite sex, I'm out of my depth. No one has ever told me what to do or how to act. So, I'm out here in the deep end with…you, and I just…don't want to get in over my head." I stare at her unblinking, unsure of what to say when she continues. "I'm not asking for a whole lot…or maybe I am." She shrugs. "Just be honest with me."

"Honesty." I nod. "I can do that."

"Can you?" Her gaze narrows. There's a fine line between curiosity and judgment and she's towing it, but her vulnerable candor makes me believe it's the former.

"Yes. I'm always honest and transparent about how things

are. It's not my fault that women want more than I'm willing to give."

"Fair." She turns and begins to make herself a cup of coffee. My eyes rake over her body lasciviously.

I want her. Whatever she's willing to give me, I want it. I want to be greedy with her. Her time. Her body. Everything. I want it all.

"Can I see you tonight?"

She turns her head to the side for me to see her profile. "Like...a date?"

"I was thinking you could come to my place...but... if you'd prefer, we can go out? I'm sure we could find somewhere outside of New Haven where no one would recognize us? I am certain neither of us need it getting back to your father."

She clears her throat. "I have class early tomorrow but...I could come over for a little while."

Thoughts of waking up and burying myself inside of Serena's no longer virgin pussy tomorrow morning comes to a halt and I nod. "That sounds good."

"What time?"

"Around eight?"

She nods as she grabs her coffee and holds it between her hands. "I'll be in my father's office...just let me know when I should be ready to go to court." She doesn't wait for a response before she's gone, and the air I didn't realize I was holding, leaves my lungs.

Seven

Serena

IF SOMEONE WOULD HAVE TOLD ME THAT WATCHING LANDON West in action would have been some sort of sexy aphrodisiac...*actually, I probably would have believed them.* Landon makes *everything* look sexy. Despite the fact that I was furiously scribbling down notes, I couldn't ignore the way my skin heated up every time he *objected* to something the opposing counsel said. Every time he made a point that left the other side scrambling in defense, I squeezed my legs together tighter. He's a brilliant lawyer, with a level of charisma that can't be taught. It's innate and all one can do is hope that by proxy the skills will rub off on them.

Now I'm thinking about him rubbing off on me.

Rubbing on me.

I cough back the tension bubbling up in my throat and I'm grateful that he's been on the phone since we emerged from the courtroom because the way I'm feeling, I might ask him to touch me right here in the middle of the hallway. To kiss me like he did last night.

So, not only am I attracted to him *physically*, but now I am attracted to him *mentally,* too.

I am so screwed.

Yes, screwed, Serena. As in let him screw you.

"What did you think?" His words interrupt my train of thought. Our eyes meet and the crooked smile I've come to love spreads across his face.

"It was so exhilarating." The words leave my mouth in a gush. "You were fantastic!" I hadn't meant to sound like a fangirl mooning over a rockstar but the way he looks at me in shock, it's safe to say he appreciates my praise. "Thank you for letting me tag along." I hold my memo pad—with all the notes I took— close to my chest as we make our way through the empty hallway.

His hand skates over my shoulders, finding my lower back and I shiver at his touch. It stops me in my tracks and he follows suit, leaving us in the middle of the hallway. He moves closer to me, close enough to remind me of his cologne and the fact that he is currently chewing spearmint gum; it makes me weak in the knees. "You are most welcome, sweetheart. I'm glad I could be there for your first time." His term of endearment warms my bones *as well as other parts of me.*

"I took so many notes." I push my glasses further on my nose and tuck a hair behind my ear. "Do…do you want to see? I'm sure you've already thought of everything, but there was one card I feel like you could have played." I fiddle with the notepad in my hand, suddenly feel stupid. *He's a smart, cunning lawyer, what could I possibly add that he hasn't even thought of?* "I…sorry." I look down, regretting my words instantly when he raises my chin to look at him.

"Why are you sorry? I'd love to see what you wrote down. Good lawyers talk a lot, great lawyers listen. Remember that, Serena." He winks.

I nod, soaking in all the advice that this man can give. We walk towards the exit and I feel like I'm floating on a cloud, when I'm suddenly brought back to Earth at the sound of my name being called.

I spin when I hear the familiar voice. "Dad! You're not going to believe—" I start when I notice the frown on his face as he gets closer.

"Serena, what are you doing here?" My father rarely gets angry. Irritated or frustrated, yes, but it takes a lot for him to get truly angry, and rarely has it ever been towards me. But seeing the look in his eye, I can sense his anger flowing out of him in waves. His tie is loose around his neck and his jacket is slung over his arm. His hair is slightly disheveled like he'd run his hands through it several times and his eyes look tired behind his glasses.

"I…Lan— Mr. West brought me," I stammer.

His eyes dart to the man next to me, and I wonder if he notices my slip of almost calling him by his first name. *He told you to call him Landon in front of your father. Relax, Serena. Your father doesn't know you kissed him. He doesn't know you're hanging out with him tonight.*

"If I thought you were ready, I would have brought you myself, Serena."

"There's nothing to be "ready" for," Landon interrupts. "She's an intern it's not like she needs to make closing remarks, P. Lighten up." He chuckles, but I hear his defensiveness and, for a moment, I let myself dwell in that.

"You throw your interns in the deep end without so much as a life raft. I'm not about to let you do the same with Serena. She's not ready," He barks at Landon.

"*She's* right here." I perk up as I point at myself. "And Dad…"

"Serena, wait outside." He gestures towards the mahogany polished door.

"Wait. What?" *Is he…dismissing me?*

"I said: Wait. Outside. I'm heading back to the office, you can ride with me." I frown, hating this chastising tone he's using. I chance a glance at Landon, but he gives nothing away as I make my way outside. I briefly think about calling Skyler to rant, but Skyler and my dad share a bond I don't quite understand.

You understand it quite perfectly, she's his favorite.

I take a deep breath trying to ignore the embarrassment that threatens to come out in the form of tears when my dad's voice interrupts me. "He's not your friend, Serena. It's not appropriate for you to just go off with random men."

His words are like a punch in the gut and I feel like the air slowly leaves my lungs. *'He's not your friend, Serena.'* "He's not exactly random, Dad. I need material for my paper, and I wasn't getting any sitting in your office like I have been all week."

"You're not interning for *him*, Serena." He runs a hand through his hair and I can already hear the implication.

"So, it wasn't that I came to court without you, but that I came with Mr. West?" *Maybe, just maybe he had more faith in me than I thought. Maybe it wasn't about wanting to keep me out of the courtroom. But just getting caught up in the charm that was Landon West.*

"It's both. You weren't ready. You still have so much to learn. And as I told you, they were both closed hearings."

"Which is fine, but his hearing wasn't. How am I going to learn if I don't experience anything?" I cross my arms, suddenly feeling emboldened to speak my mind. My dad has such little faith in me. He believes I'm this naive, sensitive, innocent wallflower that needs shelter from everything.

And maybe I am.

But now I was ready to bloom and Landon is like the sun. He was those forces of nature that I needed to blossom.

"Just promise you'll stay away from Landon. I know he's charming and his cases are sexy and intriguing," *yeah, dad, his cases,* I think, "but he's not…he's not a good guy."

I frown. *He's always spoken so highly of Landon. Where is this coming from?* "He's your friend."

"Which is why I know how he can be. He draws you in and then just…spits you out. I've seen what he's done to…*people*. I don't want him to have the opportunity to hurt you in *any* capacity."

"Dad…" I start. "He just wanted me to see some action. I was bored sitting in your office." I shake my head. "It's not a big deal."

He huffs and pinches the bridge of his nose, clearly over this conversation. "Let's go, Serena." He walks towards the adjacent garage, and I reluctantly begin to follow when something in my periphery catches my attention. Landon is standing in the doorway, leaning against the wall with a worried look on his face. He taps his phone, signaling me to check mine. I reach into my purse to retrieve it as I continue to trail after my father

LW: Did he give you a hard time? I told him it was my idea to bring you.
Me: It's fine. Did he give YOU a hard time?
LW: I can handle your father, Serena. Tell me, what did he say?

I don't respond because I'm not sure what's worse; disclosing what my father alluded to about Landon or his lack of faith in his daughter.

My room looks like a tornado hit. Clothes are strewn over every surface and every pair of shoes I own is outside the boxes I store them in. My bathroom is just as chaotic; curling wands and flat irons sit on my sink while thirty different shades of lipsticks line my counter.

"You're not helping, Zoey. How about this one?" I stand in front of my computer as I skype with my best friend, holding a dress up over my half-naked body. Zoey and I have known each other practically since birth, and she also went to UConn. She'd been royally pissed to learn that I would be living at home and not with her in the dorms or even once she moved off campus because, as she eloquently put it, I could not lose my virginity while living at Viv and P's. *Although, she used more colorful language.* But even with me living at home, Zoey and I have still remained close despite the fact that we are complete opposites.

"I didn't say I was going to help." She takes a sip of a glass of rosé next to the computer and tucks a blonde strand behind her ear. "I said I would give you a pep talk for your big night. Who gives a shit what you wear, you could wear a trench coat and a smile for God's sakes. He's going to rip it off of you when you walk in, right? Did you wax?"

"I... shaved."

"Not my first choice but whatever. As long as you're groomed." She takes another sip of her drink. "Don't be nervous."

"I'm nervous." I sink into my chair and drop my head to the desk. "I'm not ready for this."

"Yes, you are! He's hot as fuck, Rena. You should go for it.

You almost banged him in your car the other night. You want this."

"I did not almost *bang* him."

She blinks her eyes at me a few times as if she doesn't understand what I'm saying. "Okay, Rena. Look, everything is going to be fine. Don't do anything you don't feel comfortable doing. But…if you want to…go for it. You're calling the shots here, alright?" She cocks her head to the side and gives me a smile. "You've always gone after what you want. This is no different."

I take a deep breath, letting her words wash over me. I nod before holding the dress I was previously holding in front of the computer. "I don't know what to wear."

She sighs and lets her head fall back with a loud groan. "I already said this isn't my lane."

"What good are you? You're supposed to be my best friend."

"I would wear soccer shorts and a t-shirt. I already told you, I'm not the one to ask." She points at the screen towards me. "Your hair looks good."

I look at my hair that I haven't touched since I got out of the shower. "Are you serious?"

"What! Less is more, Rena. He's an adult. Like a real adult. You don't have to do…" she points at the screen, "all that."

"Fine. Should I forego underwear?" I ask.

"Now we're talkin'!" she cheers as she holds her glass up to toast me.

Despite Zoey's '*do less everything is going to be fine,*' advice, I'm still nervous. Beyond nervous.

I'm walking up to Landon's house with a bottle of wine, in a sweater dress over a pair of leggings and ballet flats. I thought about baking him something, but given that I spent most of the evening trying to find what to wear and removing every stray hair from my body, I figured wine would suffice. I'm halfway up the path when his door flies open and he's walking towards me. His hair is slightly wet, like he's recently showered, and he's wearing a pair of gray sweatpants and a white t-shirt that shows off his glorious muscles. I'm used to seeing him in a suit, so seeing him severely dressed down is making my mouth water.

I lick my lips, as my eyes skate over his crotch and on cue, I see something rise underneath the gray pants. "Hi." I smile as I hand him a bottle of wine. "I brought wine."

"You didn't have to bring anything." He leans down and presses a kiss to the corner of my mouth and the smell of soap, clean laundry, and *man* floods my senses, and I've instantly learned what my favorite smell in the world is. "Come in, I have something in the oven that needs to come out."

I stop in my tracks and my eyes widen. "You cooked?"

He stops walking and turns to looks at me and then at his watch. "It's eight. Of course, I cooked. We weren't going out, and this is a date, is it not?"

A date! "Well, we hadn't…I mean, I just…" *I thought I was only coming over for sex…not food.* "Right, yes."

He grabs my hand interlacing our fingers and runs his lips over them. I almost combust, dying for another taste of his lips on mine as he leads me into his townhouse.

Although this space is supposedly only temporary, it is well furnished and appears to be well lived in. Pictures of him and his son line the walls of the foyer and the kitchen and living areas are fully furnished. A fire roars in the fireplace in the corner of the living room and I hear the sounds of what I believe to be Frank Sinatra playing quietly. *This man is good.*

"Wine?" he asks. I take a seat at the kitchen table, feeling so out of my element I'm sure that the ability to sit upright will leave me at any moment.

"Okay. Do you need any help?" I ask. *Cooking I can do. Cooking is easy. It is this that is hard.*

"Nope, all done."

"You did this by yourself?" I crane my neck to see what he pulls out of the oven and I'm shocked to see a baked ziti. "You made something Italian?"

"Don't look so surprised, Bambi. I'm a man of many talents." He winks. "Your mom gave Jana the recipe a few years back…" He shrugs. "I like it." Hearing his ex's name fall from his lips sends a surge of jealousy through me that I don't expect. *Calm down, Serena.*

I raise an eyebrow at him. "You think *I'll* like it?"

"I'm sure of it." He sits next to me as he lets the food cool and pours us both a glass of wine. "I'm glad you're here."

"Me too." I fiddle with my glasses nervously as I wait for him to make a move. A move I know is coming. He strokes my cheek gently and leans in. I expect him to plant his lips on mine, but he just rubs his nose against mine and presses a kiss to my cheek. I let out a sigh when he gets up again.

"Your dad had quite a lot to say earlier."

"What did he say to you?" I ask, the sweet moment forgotten as my curiosity gets the best of me.

"He asked me to stay away from you. Says I'm a bad influence."

"Whatever could make him say that?" I roll my eyes and giggle, and he shoots me a pointed glare.

"What does that mean?"

I gulp and stare at the glass of red wine that I'd only had a few sips of. *Shit, I'm already feeling it?* "I…I don't know."

"Sure, you do." He raises an eyebrow at me and I raise one back.

"Landon, just because I don't believe the rumors necessarily doesn't mean they don't exist."

"And if I said the rumors were true?"

I shrug. "It's your business." I look up at him and give him a small smile. "I don't think any less of you."

He prepare our plates and sets one in front of me before taking a seat to my right. "You're not like most girls."

"I know." I look down at my food, unsure of what his exact intentions are behind that comment.

"Serena look at me." I do as he says and meet his eyes. "Baby, that's a good thing."

We fall into a comfortable conversation, talking about everything and nothing while we eat my mother's baked ziti. I help him clean the kitchen before he pulls me into the living room and we settle in front of the fireplace. *Okay, this is it, Serena. Be calm. You can do this. You remember how good he felt.* Our backs are against the couch, our legs intertwined and that familiar feeling takes over my body. Because I'm on my second glass of wine and feeling bold, I broach the subject I probably shouldn't.

"Can I ask what happened? With…ummm…Jana?"

He stares at the fire for a second before turning to me, a cold look in his eye that I know isn't meant for me. "Can I not answer?"

"You don't have to. There's just a few different versions of what happened floating around the office." I take a tentative sip. "I was just wondering."

"A lot of office gossip about me, huh?"

"You give people something to talk about. My father certainly doesn't. And Frank is kind of boring."

"Jana isn't worth our time." He nuzzles my cheek. "I want to know about you."

"There's not much to know about me."

"I think that's false."

I change the subject again. *I don't want to talk about me.* "What about your son? How is he doing…all things considering?"

He narrows his eyes at me before turning towards the fire. "Griff is…" he takes a long sip of his wine, "he hates me."

"I find that hard to believe…" I whisper when he doesn't say anything for a few moments.

"No, he does. He blames me for everything. The divorce. His DUI."

"That's stupid. You didn't make him drive under the influence. I'm sure you would have gone to pick him up wherever he was."

"In a heartbeat." He pulls my glass of wine from me. "And if you're going to keep drinking, I'm not going to let you drive either, young lady."

"I've only had two glasses!"

"And you're this tiny." He holds up his pinky finger and shakes his head. "I'll take you home later when you're ready to go."

"But then my car will still be here."

"I'll take you home in your car, and then take an Uber back."

"You said Ubers were for drunk kids or…whatever."

"For you, I'll make an exception." He taps my nose with his index finger and I giggle.

"Well maybe…" I trail off. "Maybe I can stay here and

leave in the morning?" My sex thumps in response and I take a sip of my wine to try and calm my nerves.

"I'd love for you to stay…if you want." *Was Landon West… nervous?* The look in his eyes makes me believe he's never been in this position before, and he is also out of his depth.

"I want."

Eight

Landon

THERE'S A SPECIAL PLACE IN HELL FOR PEOPLE LIKE ME. *MEN like me.* For men that let things get too far with women they shouldn't touch in the first place. *What am I doing? Is Olivia, right?* Did I get such a hard-on for young pussy that I'm willing to take P's daughter's virginity? *Shit, this is so fucked up.* I scratch my jaw and shoot her a sideways glance to find her eyeing me over the tops of her glasses. She peeks up at me through her lashes and for a brief moment I've forgotten that she has no experience. Because *that* look she's giving me is one of a seasoned veteran.

"What are you thinking about?" she asks, and I try to ignore the breathiness of her voice. *Fuck. Is she seducing me?* Her hand reaches up and traces my jaw gently, ghosting her tips over my lips and I resist the urge to suck them into my mouth.

"I've…" I clear my throat, preparing to say the words that may have her walking out my front door without another look back. "I've done some pretty shitty things in my past, Serena. I've hurt…women, not on purpose." I close my eyes, preparing myself for her response to the brutal honesty. "*Sometimes on purpose, but mostly just by being myself.*" I look at her and she's just staring at me with that doe-eyed look that makes my dick hard and my heart soft.

"You don't have to treat me like my father does, Landon."

I narrow my gaze at her, wondering where she's going with that.

"I certainly do not."

"My father underestimates me. He thinks I'm not ready for anything. That I'll need him and Mom to hold my hand my whole life. I'll admit I was scared at first. But what eighteen year old isn't scared about leaving home? It's been four years and I'm ready to spread my wings and fly from the nest. So, you don't have to give me a warning about...*you*. I'm a big girl, and I can make my own decisions. I'm here, which means I want to be. Yes, I'm a little nervous about..." she clears her throat and her face turns a delicious shade of pink, *"that,* but I want this. You told me to ask for what I want. Well, I want... you."

My dick is painfully hard hearing her confident speech about what she wants. *That she wants me.* I'm used to women beating around the bush, playing hard to get or coy or not being transparent with their feelings. Her honesty is refreshing and, frankly, it makes me want to rip her clothes off of her and impale her with my dick. "Fuck, Serena." I pull her to straddle me and she sinks down into my lap, shifting to get comfortable. "What did I tell you about that?" I groan as I steady her hips before she causes my dick to burst in my pants.

"It feels...good." Her gaze is hooded, and her lips part as her breathing begins to accelerate. I trace her skin trying to memorize every feature on her beautiful face. The freckle on her nose, how perfectly defined her lips are, the traces of honey and amber that are in her hazel eyes. She is so beautiful. A beautiful blank canvas that she is asking me to paint.

She presses her hands to my chest and leans in closer. "I never thought I would be the one talking *you* off the ledge." She giggles.

"You're not. I'm not…I'm just soaking you in."

"Can I ask you something?" Her eyes are warm and genuine, and it makes me want to tell her everything. I nod, keeping my eyes fixed on hers as she slides off of me and I sit up. "Why doesn't your son live here…with you?" Her brows furrow slightly, and I wonder if she's trying to think of the right way to phrase what she has to say. "You have the space, and I saw some of his things in the spare room. But he doesn't live here? I would just think a sixteen year old boy would want to live with his dad."

My face falls and I feel that familiar feeling flooding through my veins, hurt mixed with rage mixed with confusion. I want Griffin around and it kills me that he doesn't want to spend time with me. I'm angry at his mother for making that impossible, and him for allowing himself to be brainwashed. I'd been there for him his whole life, and now I am suddenly cast aside over lies his mother has told him. "It's complicated." She gives me a look that says '*try anyway.*' "Actually, it's quite simple. He'd rather live with his mom. He's mad at me right now."

"Because you can't fix the DUI? That's not fair."

"Not just because of the DUI. There's a few other reasons."

"Have you tried talking to him?"

"Of course, I have." I'd shown up at school, his after-school job, his football practices. "He won't talk to me."

"Try harder, Landon. Kids want someone to fight for them. They want a father that cares enough to fix the problems between them even when we act like spoiled brats. Even when we tell you that you'll never understand us. We want you to *try.*" *Is she speaking from personal experience? She can't be...Preston and Viv adore her and Skyler. They have the perfect family.*

"You don't understand, Serena..."

"There's nothing to *understand.* He's your son and he needs you whether he thinks so or not. He might push you away, but he wants you to push back. Whatever it is, you can fix it. You'll regret it later if you don't."

Her words feel like a punch in the gut. *Am I failing him by not pushing back?* "His mother has fed him...a bunch of lies. Put him in the middle of us." I clear my throat.

She climbs into my lap and buries her face in my neck and I'm not sure if it's supposed to comfort me or *her.* But I feel tension leaving my body in waves as she snuggles in closer. "Tell him the truth. Don't let her villainize you. Have you even tried?"

"She has him so brainwashed. Told him I cheated on her. That I'm the reason we are getting divorced. I'm the reason our family is breaking up. Kids resent that kind of shit." I swallow back the anger I feel towards my father who'd walked out on us when I was fifteen after a slew of affairs. *That's different. You're nothing like that asshole.*

She pulls back to look at me and her lip trembles slightly; her empathy astounds me. "I'm sorry," she says softly. Her glossy, hazel eyes are almost brown as they shine with a level of sadness that I wasn't expecting. It's almost as if she feels the pain I feel.

"She's the one that had the affair. but I would never tell him that."

"Why not?"

"Because I don't want to pass my issues with Jana onto to

my son. That's not fair. And for the most part…she's a decent mother."

"That's admirable, Landon."

"I don't want him to hate her. But is it so wrong to not want him to hate me either?"

She doesn't say anything, she just presses her lips to mine gently, sliding her tongue through my lips as her hand drifts down my chest, rubbing circles into it. It's a different kind of answer.

It isn't pity.

It isn't advice.

It's an escape.

Smooth skin that I can't stop kissing warms underneath my lips as I continue to pepper kisses along her neck and the swell of her soft breasts. She'd pulled her sweater off the second the kissing turned into aggressive making out and heavy petting and, now, Serena is on her back beneath me in only her bra and her leggings. She moans just as my tongue runs along the edge of her bra and the sound has a direct line to my dick. I'm seconds from yanking the cup down and freeing her breasts from the confines of the fabric when she speaks. "Take your shirt off."

I sit up and pull my shirt off over my head, desperate to get my lips back on her body. "Wait, let me see you!" she says, holding her hands out to stop me from coming closer.

"Fuck, you're killing me, Serena. I need my fucking lips on you." *For longer than one night.*

She doesn't say anything. She just gapes at my chest before darting her gaze up to my eyes. "Your body is…incredible."

Her fingertips run up each of my abs before she shoots me a devilish grin. "I want to be on top."

"Uhhhh," I stutter. It's one thing for me to be on top, so I can somewhat control how much friction her pussy makes with my cock, but I don't need her dry humping the fuck out of me while we make out. "No, Serena."

"Why?"

"Because your ass moves around too much." *So? Aren't we fucking her tonight?* My cock has been screaming at me since she sat in my lap and we kissed like teenagers in my driveway, and he doesn't seem to be thrilled over the fact that I keep pumping the breaks.

"Please," she pouts.

I let out a breath, praying to whoever might be up there to have some mercy on me, but before I can answer her, she's sitting straight up and pushing me to lie down. She leans down and presses a kiss to one of my abs before letting her tongue dart out to lick the muscle. "Serena."

"Landon." She groans as she straddles my pelvis and begins to move against my cock. *Fuck. This is what I didn't want to happen. I am ready to fucking blow.* She continues to rub her body against me, using my chest for leverage as she moves up and back on my covered shaft. "It's so hard." She breathes out, her eyes fluttering shut and her head flying back. *Holy shit, is she going to come?*

Fuck, I actually might.

I squeeze my eyes shut, as my cock pulses underneath her covered pussy. "Serena, enough." I grit out. "I'm not letting you come like this. I need to be inside of you."

She raises her head and looks down at me nervously. "Maybe... maybe I'm not ready for sex yet," she whispers. "I feel like I want to explore other things before I take that step."

"You want my mouth on your pussy." I raise an eyebrow at her and I'm shocked that the blush doesn't find her cheeks in response.

"I want...that." She nods. *I'll have you saying pussy by the time it's all over, baby.* She bites her bottom lip and before she can say another word I have her on her back and her leggings ripped from her body. Stark white lace adorns the special space between her legs and I can already smell her arousal wafting through the air around me. "I want to bottle your fucking scent, Serena." She doesn't say anything but begins to breathe deeply. "Don't be nervous," I whisper.

"I'm not. I'm just...anxious."

"Because you want it so bad."

"Yes."

I ignore her pussy for a moment, knowing that the second it comes into view, I'll become obsessed with it for God knows how long and I'd like to maintain some semblance of sanity. "These are pretty," I tell her as I finger her satin bra that matches her panties. "It matches." I reach behind her and unclip her bra, letting it slide down her arms. I search her eyes for any hesitation but she only nods her head. I'm vaguely aware that she's rubbing her legs together, probably feeling as keyed up as I do in this moment.

"Your breasts are incredible, Serena." They're porn star tits; round and supple, and perfect for all the depraved things I want to do to her. The second my hands find her nipples she shivers and lets out a guttural moan as I rub my thumbs over them both.

"Oh God, that feels good."

"This will feel even better," I tell her as I lean down and suck one into my mouth. I've had my fair share of breasts in my mouth, but it's safe to say none of them tasted like

Serena's. She tastes like honey and it makes my mouth water. It makes me want to spend the rest of my life attached to them. She lets out a whimper and then a shriek when I bite down gently. She grabs the back of my head and pushes me further onto her breast. "Tell me how it feels, baby."

"So good. Please don't stop."

I don't know how long I've been worshipping her breasts, but when I pull away there are hickeys. *Everywhere.* "Fuck… Serena, I'm…I got a little carried away."

She looks down and then up at me, shaking her head. "It's okay. You're the only one who will be looking at them. I think it's kind of hot that you were so lost in the moment." She bites that fucking lip *again,* and I swear she's just doing this shit to torture me.

I lean down and rain gentle kisses on the fresh red bruises that will be purple by tomorrow. I run my tongue over each of them to soothe the bite from my teeth. I pull back after some time to stare down at her practically naked body.

"Did you wear these white underwear to tease me?" I ask her as I move down to her pussy in preparation for doing one of the many things I've been fantasizing about doing to Serena since she walked into the office earlier this week.

"No."

"You sure?"

She giggles. "Okay, perhaps."

I kiss her stomach, running my lips slowly across the top of her panties and then down the slit, placing a kiss right on her clit that I could tell was peeking out from its hood and she hisses. "You're good at this whole seduction thing, you know that?"

I grip her hips and raise them slightly to meet my mouth. "Really? I'm trying really hard to exercise restraint right now.

Trust me, all I want to do is dive right in and eat you like you're my last meal." I nuzzle the space between her thighs, relishing in her scent.

"Why don't you?"

"Because this is your first time. I want it to be special. If it wasn't, trust me, I would have bent you over my desk in my office already."

"It'll be special whatever way you do it. Because *it's you*. You're special."

Fuck, she's innocent. So sweet and kind-hearted.

I wasn't expecting for her to say anything that would render me speechless. Especially while she was practically naked and I could see the arousal glistening between her legs behind her panties. But her words stop me and all I want to do is pull her into my arms and protect her from all the bad shit in the world.

"Serena…"

"Sorry, did I totally kill the mood?"

"No, baby. You didn't." *You've been the only reason I've been in a good mood for the last few days.*

And just as I begin to slide her panties down her legs for a taste of what's behind it, I have a brief, fleeting thought that just maybe I won't fuck this up.

"Your scent is…mouthwatering," I tell her as I meet her shy gaze.

I open her folds, exposing her wet sex and slide my tongue through them, flicking her clit letting her sweet taste coat my tongue.

"Oh my God, Landon," she whispers and I already feel her quivering around my tongue. *Well, that certainly didn't take long.* I wrap my lips around her clit, sucking the hard nub into my mouth and she *loses* it, clamping her legs around my head.

"Fuck!" The word leaves her mouth so suddenly, that I almost stop what I'm doing. And if she wasn't on the precipice of an orgasm, I would have stopped and congratulated her on what I believe to be her first swear word.

But I need her sweetness that I know will melt in my mouth like the most decadent dessert. I smile to myself as I remember the first time I had an orgasm. I was locked in the bathroom for the majority of my thirteenth year, so Serena has a lot of catching up to do. Her hands find my hair and she pulls, *hard* and I groan in response. I was no stranger to eating pussy and I know that I could drive a woman wild with a flick of my tongue. The violent shudders of Serena's first orgasm coursing through her are badges of honor I plan to wear with pride.

I sit up, licking her juices from my lips and swallowing them down as she comes down from her high. "You're so good at that…Wow. What reason would any woman have to be mad at you?" She giggles and sits up slightly, her long hair falling wildly all over her face.

I ignore her comment, because quite frankly women had about a million reasons to be angry at me, and none of them could be fixed with my mouth. "You said fuck."

She frowns and pulls her hair over one shoulder. "I did not."

"Yes, you did. When you came."

She bites her bottom lip and looks at the ceiling. "Did I?"

"Yes, ma'am. In an exclamatory fashion."

"Well, you did say when a woman is thoroughly…umm *that*, she would start swearing." She grins.

She ain't seen nothing yet.

"Trust me, baby, you are *far* from thoroughly fucked."

Nine

Landon

SOFT HANDS AND KISSES ROUSE ME FROM SLEEP AT WHAT I assume to be an unGodly hour if my alarm hasn't gone off yet. "Landon, I have to go," she whispers against my lips before she peppers kisses along my jaw.

I grumble in response to her words knowing that it means there's no time for me to taste her. "Why didn't you wake me sooner? I want to make you come again." I pull her warm body underneath mine, and I'm grateful that she's still naked. Not surprisingly, seeing as how I still had a vice grip on her body when I woke up.

"I don't have time," she whines as she looks at the clock next to my bed. "I have to be in class in less than two hours and I still have to go home and grab my things." I press my cock that's hardening by the second into her naked sex and she whimpers in response. "Landon..."

"Will I see you later?" I ask. I press my lips to her neck and grind harder against her, causing a rush of air to leave her lungs.

Somewhere deep inside of me, I feel the breakthrough forming in response to my question. *You actually care, huh? That's new.*

"Yes, I'll be in this afternoon."

"Come to my office when you get there."

"Landon…I can't just…"

"Come to my office, Serena. I mean it." I pull back and give her a look that lets her know I'm serious.

She shakes her head, a sneaky smile playing on her lips. "You're going to get us in trouble."

I ignore her comment, knowing I plan to keep her out of the line of fire. "Text me when you get to campus…" I start. "Actually, text me when you get home too."

She nods. "Okay." I let her leave the bed and follow her with my eyes. Even under the low light of the room, she glows and her naked body calls out to me on the most primal level. I watch as she grabs her clothes from the chair and slides them on in what seems to be slow motion. *Tease.* "You're staring."

"You're beautiful."

I stand up and walk over towards her, but her eyes are fixed about four feet south of my eyes. She bites her lip and my cock jumps in response. Once I'm standing right in front of her, I lift her chin to meet my gaze. "See something you like?"

She nods. "I want…I want to see it."

"Now?"

She nods. "Please? You saw everything last night. It's only fair."

"So, you want me to take it out for you to look at it? Are you trying to kill me, Serena?"

"Just a peek."

"You're a tease, you know that?" Serena had tried to get my pants off last night, on more than one occasion, but I wanted last night to be about her. And I wasn't sure that I trusted myself to be completely naked around her while *she* was completely naked. I didn't want her to feel pressured to do anything and a hard dick can be pretty persuasive.

She looks up at me, giving me that look that says *you're going to do it anyway, don't argue with me* as her hands find the waistband of my sweats. Her cool fingers touch my warm skin just above my briefs and I shudder. "Serena…" My voice is raspy and deep, both from sleep and this hunger for her that's growing more aggressive by the second, making me feel like I'm hanging on by an actual thread.

I watch with bated breath as she lowers herself to the ground, sliding my sweats down to my ankles. I can feel her breath on my thighs and I don't want her to feel like she has to do this. "Baby, you don't—"

"Shhh," she interrupts me. "I've never seen a penis before." She blurts out.

"They don't look that different than the ones in porn." I chuckle. "I mean mine will be bigger." I smirk.

She swallows. "Well…I don't watch porn…ever. I mean, I've never seen a pornographic film."

A film? God, she's cute. "Never?"

"I mean maybe in a biology class or something?"

"No, I mean…you've never watched porn?"

"No?" She looks up at me. Her hands find my briefs and before I can say anything she's tugged them down my legs and my erection juts out, almost hitting her in the face as it bobs up and down.

Her mouth drops open and it takes every amount of restraint I have not to inch my cock towards it. *Fucking hell, Landon. Don't you dare.*

"It's so beautiful," she says and I can't help the smile that comes from her compliment. "I want to touch it," she murmurs. It's not a question and for a brief moment I wonder if she's going to ask how to do so.

Just as I'm about to instruct her on what to do, her hand finds the bottom of my shaft and she drags it up to the tip. "Fuuuuuuuck." I groan. "Serena."

"Does that feel good?"

"Yes." I groan again.

She does it again, adding more pressure this time and rubbing her thumb across the tip. I watch with fascination as she collects the beads of cum that form on my tip and slides it between her lips.

"Jesus Christ, Serena."

"I want to try something."

"If you put your mouth on my dick, you're going to be late for class."

"I'm willing to risk it." She scrunches her nose and gives me a grin. "You gave me countless orgasms last night and you wouldn't even let me touch you."

"Because I knew your limits and I didn't want to test them."

"I was nervous. I didn't think I was ready, but I woke up this morning and... I'm not so nervous anymore." *Probably because she was rubbing her ass against me half the night.* She bites her bottom lip and slides her tongue up my cock, leaving her eyes trained on me. *Where the fuck did she learn that?*

"Serena...I can't fuck you...now. Not while you're rushing to be somewhere else. I want to take my time. I want to worship you. Discover each and every one of your sounds and tastes and smells and *fuck*, I want to do so much to you."

She looks up at me, her eyes bright and sparkling as the words fall from her lips. "I want to make you come." Those six words have pre-cum leaking from my tip and dripping down my shaft.

"Fuck."

Her tongue catches the drop and drags up my member before closing her lips around the tip and sliding her whole mouth down my dick. Her hands find my thighs just as my hand finds her hair. I pull it off of her face and into a makeshift ponytail as I watch her suck my dick like she was made for it.

Do not come already. All the thoughts leave my mind the second I feel her teeth grazing the skin and nails digging into my ass.

"Serena...Fuck. Can I come in your mouth?" I ask praying that the answer is yes. I need a piece of me inside of her.

She nods her head. "Yes," she says, her mouth still full of my cock and the vibrations send a jolt of electricity slithering up my spine.

Normally, I'd push further into a woman's mouth. Make them gag and their eyes water. That visual, a woman on her knees, with mascara streaming down their cheeks as they choke on my dick gets me to the finish line the fastest. But with Serena, I let her control the pace. Her eyes haven't left mine almost the entire time and it makes me wonder if she, like the others were desperate for my praise too.

Fuck. Did she have the same issues all the other ones have?

For the first time, that bothers me. I don't want her to want me because I remind her of her father. Because she wants love and praise that she never receives from him.

She pulls away, letting my dick fall from between her lips. "You went somewhere else. I could see it in your eyes. Or maybe...maybe I'm not doing it right?" Her eyes are sad and I can see the worry behind them, thinking that she's disappointed me.

Fuck, I forgot she was looking at me. "No, baby you were doing perfectly."

"Really?" Her eyes light up and a smile finds her lips. I know that look.

Fuck fuck fuck.

What did you expect? She's twenty-one and insanely gorgeous. She's got her whole life ahead of her. What other reason would she have for being with you?

You are her rebellious phase.

Her cry for attention.

Attention from her real father.

"Baby, I don't want you to be late for class," I tell her as I cup her face lightly.

"You...you want me to stop? I mean you didn't come." She leans forward and grabs my dick again.

Just let her finish.

"Sweetheart, I promise you can later. I have to hit the gym before I go in anyway."

"You'd rather workout than..." She looks at my dick and then up at me with a cheeky smirk.

No? But your daddy issues are showing and it's fucking with my head.

Why? It's not like you want her for more than just sex...

You're not capable of more than that.

Fuck.

A million thoughts run through my head and I can only imagine what my face looks like in response. I can't do this with her staring at me.

"Come to my office when you get in." I help her to her feet and pull my boxers and sweats up.

"Okay."

I throw on a shirt and follow her downstairs and out to her car. Judging by the placement of the sun, I would say it's about 7 AM. She reaches up on her tiptoes and wraps her arms around my neck and I can hear her inhaling my scent. "Thanks for letting me stay."

I kiss the side of her head, wondering how in the hell I'm going to make sense of the feelings I have for her. When she pulls back, she presses her lips to mine in a kiss so needy and deep that I can't help but succumb to the pleasure. I press her against her car, tangling my hands in her hair and kissing her like I don't have nosy neighbors that already know too much about my life. I can taste my cock on her tongue, reminding me that I'm the only one that's been there and it awakens the caveman inside of me struggling to claw it's way out. When I pull away, I can actually see the stars in her eyes before I let my eyes drift down to her swollen and wet lips and just like that I'm hard as a rock.

"Bye Landon." She giggles before she disappears into her car and pulls out of my driveway. I doubt she's even to the end of my street before I'm back inside with my hand wrapped around my dick.

A timid knock on my door has me out of my seat instantly, despite the conference call I'm on. Holding the phone to my ear I open the door, prepared for Serena to walk through. I haven't quite come to terms with what exactly I'm feeling, but I know I want to be near her. I know that even if I can't be with her, I can help her work through these *issues*. I can give her what she wants. I can give her...*me*. And when she's finished, I will let her go.

It's just the chase. The forbidden fruit. Like Olivia said.

Speak of the Devil.

I'm instantly irritated when I see Olivia standing at the door. "I'm on a call, what?" I snap at her.

"Your files." She holds them in front of my face. "Valerie asked me to give them to you."

Bullshit. Valerie lives by the notion of 'if you want something done right, do it yourself.' "What did you pay her to let you come hand deliver this?" I snatch them from her and walk away, hoping she gets the message.

"You're so tense." She purrs.

"I'm on a call," I bark at her, hoping she gets the message that she needs to get the hell out of my office.

"You used to eat my pussy during those so-called *calls.*"

"*Used* to."

"Look, I get you're pissed. I was in a weird headspace that day. I don't want to end this."

Who didn't see this coming?

I continue looking down at the files she delivered like she isn't standing in front of me with a sign screaming, *"Please fuck me, Daddy, I'm sorry."*

"Miss Barrett, that part of our relationship is over."

"Oh, come on, you remember how good it was, don't you?" Her voice suddenly sounds like nails on a chalkboard and makes me long for the softer voice that was whispering in my ear all night.

"Olivia, you were right. It's best we end it now."

She crosses her arms in front of her chest, pushing her breasts upwards and, for the first time, it does nothing for me. "You're so obvious, you know that?"

I ignore her comment, not wanting to entertain her bullshit. I stand up in preparation to remove her from my office when she continues. "You have such a hard-on for Mr. Mitchell's daughter. Do you really want to go down that road?" *This shit again? Am I really that fucking obvious?*

No, regrettably, Olivia just knows what it looks like when you're into someone.

Although, I never looked at Olivia the way I look at Serena.

I look at her, furious. "Green is an ugly color on you, Olivia," I try to reign in the anger even if she is pissing me off because I know that underneath the jealousy is hurt and the sting of rejection.

A flash of hurt crosses her face and she takes a step back. "I've seen the way she looks at you too, Landon. You're not good for her. You need to stop whatever it is you're doing."

My thoughts of worrying about her feelings fly out the window. "Need I remind you, that I am not only your boss but a partner at this firm and you are way the fuck out of line."

My words seem to remind her that while, yes, she is my ex-lover, she is also a subordinate. And thus, I am only going to let her get away with so much. "Leave her alone, Landon. Before you hurt her like the rest of us." She turns her teary gaze away from me and storms out of the office without another glance.

After Olivia's dramatic exit, I'm in the shittiest mood. A shitty mood that would have instantly improved by seeing Serena's sweet face except *she isn't fucking here yet.* She'd texted me when she left campus, but that was over an hour ago, and it shouldn't take this long to get here. I pick up the phone to call her, perfectly aware that my obsessive boyfriend traits are showing, but I want to know where she is. *Now.*

"Hey."

"Where are you?" I demand. "You should be here by now."

"I'm…here." She sounds almost bored, and it pisses me the fuck off.

"Here where?" I demand.

"My dad's office."

What the fuck?

"For how long?"

"About thirty minutes."

"Didn't I tell you to come to me when you got here?" She's silent and I wonder if P is in there with her. "Are you not alone?" *I could have sworn he was in a meeting but maybe it got canceled.*

"I am."

Oh, fuck that. I'm out of my office, closing my door behind me before I can change my mind. I move down the hall, and I'm through his office door all within the span of a minute. She blinks at me, the phone still to her ear and lets it fall, ending our phone call. "Why didn't you tell me you were here? Why didn't you come to my office like I asked?"

"You were…busy when I got here."

"Busy?" I close the door behind me, grateful that her father's assistant isn't sitting outside of his office. *Doesn't she know she could have interrupted whatever I was doing?*

"Olivia was there." She clears her throat. "And I wasn't sure if it was smart for me to show my face given the nature of your conversation." She swallows and looks towards the open windows. "She wants you."

"I don't want her…I want you."

Her neck snaps towards me. "I'm not jealous, I was just stating a fact."

She's not jealous? "You're sure you're not jealous?"

"Did I love her comment about you eating her out?" She winces. "Not particularly, but, no, Landon, I'm not jealous."

"Well, let's get one thing straight," I growl as I make strides across the room towards her. "I am the jealous type. I'm also the possessive type. So, if I tell you to come to me, you *come*," I tell her. She looks vastly different from this morning when I left her. Her hair is down in loose waves and she's dressed in a black and beige color block skirt that accentuates her legs. I pull her to her feet and press my lips to hers, desperate for her taste.

"Lan—" she moans. "My dad…"

"Your dad is in a meeting on the fourth floor for at least another hour." I press her against the wall, kissing her like my life depends on it. "I need to eat your pussy again."

"Here?!" she squeaks, and like the man possessed that she's slowly turning me into, my hand is already up her skirt before she can protest.

I skim her panties with one finger, and my cock twitches when I feel how soaked she is. "You're so wet," I whisper. "Holy fuck." I lift her in my arms and carry her to Preston's desk and sit her on top, spreading her legs in the process.

Not here, Landon. Not fucking here, my subconscious begs, but I ignore it. I ignore everything from my skeptical thoughts earlier, to where we are, to whose daughter this is as I lift her skirt around her waist, rip her panties from her cunt and spread her lips to see her wet sex. My eyes devour her folds that are glistening with arousal, committing the stunning visual to memory.

It pulses under my gaze and I find myself in a trance as I watch her clench. "You make me so fucking reckless," I murmur just before I press my lips to her slippery folds.

"Oh God." She throws a hand over her mouth as she uses the other to press my head harder against her. "I thought about this all class." She moans before she looks down, locking eyes with me. "I could barely focus."

"You make *me* lose all focus, Bambi. I can't stop thinking about you."

She locks her legs around my neck and leans back as I continue to fuck her with my mouth... *on her father's desk.*

Yep. I have a one-way ticket straight to hell.

I look up just in time to see her throw her head back and grab her breast through her blouse.

But what a way to go.

"I'm so close."

I slide my tongue through her opening, rubbing her walls. "Tell me how bad you want it, Bambi. *Beg* for it."

"Please." She moans. "I need it."

"Tell me how bad you want *me*," I demand. I'd never asked a woman to express her need so explicitly. I never needed to know how badly a woman wanted me. But with Serena, it's different. I crave her praise, her attention, her *fucking everything.*

It's been less than a month and I'm in way over my head with this girl.

She grabs my head, locking eyes with me and pulling me away from her sex much to my reluctance. For a moment, neither of us says anything, just letting our eyes do all the talking and I feel my dick hardening under her gaze. "I've never wanted something as badly as I want you." Her cheeks turn pink. "And I want you to be my first." She bites her bottom lip, trying to hide the shy smile spreading across her lips.

In less than twenty-four hours, I've watched this woman begin to transform in front of my eyes and it is quite possibly the most beautiful transition I've ever witnessed. *Had she ever felt comfortable asking for what she wanted until she met me?*

Had anyone even asked her what she wanted?

I give a final kiss to her pussy before I stand up, towering over her and I rub her sexy panties over my face to collect the arousal from her pussy.

Her eyes darken and she nods her head. *"Like now."* She grins and I chuckle, wondering how she could think losing her virginity on her father's desk in the middle of the workday is a good idea.

"How about you come over later?" I brush my nose against hers before I help her off the desk.

She pouts, actually pouts and it's perhaps the cutest thing I've ever seen. *Probably because she hasn't come.* She smooths her hair down and straightens her skirt and for a brief second, I consider giving her back her panties. *Nah.* I think as I pocket them. "Can we go continue this in your office?"

I laugh and head towards the door with her in tow when it swings open. My mind and my dick are already back in my office with Serena, so it takes a minute for me to register that her father is standing in the doorway.

Fuck.

Ten

Landon

I WATCH AS MY BEST FRIEND GOES THROUGH A RANGE OF emotions, from confusion to worry to anger. The anger is troubling, and I find myself angling myself in front of Serena to shield her from whatever her father is feeling in this moment.

"Serena Valentina Mitchell..." He steps into the room, closing the door behind him and Serena takes a tentative step back like all children do when parents use their full name. Her eyes dart to mine before turning back to him. Preston is the lawyer that doesn't lose his cool; I'm the hothead and Frank is somewhere in-between. But right now, Preston looks like he's ready to lose it. "Where in God's name have you been?"

"Ummm, school?" She gives him a look, like *where do you think,*" and the sass in her voice makes my dick hard.

"Not today, young lady. Last night! Your mother was beside herself when she woke up this morning and you weren't at home. Where were you?"

I try to remain unfazed, like I'm not guilty of having her naked and writhing underneath me for half the night. "Oh, I stayed at Zoey's." She shrugs, the lie falling from her lips so easily.

He runs a hand over his forehead before he makes his way across the room and drops into his chair. "You're always good about telling us when you're not coming home. We were worried, Serena."

"Dad, I'm twenty-one. The point of me living in the guest house is to give me some semblance of independence," she argues, and I resist the urge to praise her for standing up for herself.

"You can still let us know when you won't be home so we won't worry. You're more responsible than this, Rena."

I want to tell him to lay off, that Serena is an adult, and it's time for everyone to accept that and stop letting her use him and Viv as a crutch, but I figure this is probably not the best time. "Valerie has some things for you to do, can you go see her?" He points towards the door and I'm instantly pissed at how quickly he dismisses her.

She looks up at me and even in the brief glance I can see the hurt, the annoyance, and perhaps even slight embarrassment. "Sure, Dad," she says before she's gone.

The door has barely even clicked before I hear his voice. "Be glad you don't have girls. I swear her and Sky are going to kill me."

"Your girls are perfect, P, and they don't hate your guts. We can trade if you want." I had only meant that I wish I had a better relationship with my child, like he had with Skyler and Serena, but now the thought of Serena calling me Daddy sends a spark to my dick that I wish I could ignore. *I'm already fucking Serena Mitchell up enough as it is, let's not go down that road.*

"And what are you doing in my office, anyway?"

"I came in here looking for you. I thought maybe your meeting would be over." My lie is seamless.

"With my door closed?" I know every single one of Preston's cues. Despite the even tone, I can hear the accusations in his voice and I know his blood pressure is rising the second he slides his glasses from his face. He narrows his eyes at me and crosses his arms. "You know I will actually murder you, right?"

Play it the fuck cool. "Excuse me?"

He strums his fingers in perfect rhythm on his desk. "You touch one hair on Serena's head, and I will end you."

"You're losing your mind, Preston."

"And you're reckless and you have no regard for anyone but yourself."

Whoa, hold up. "What the fuck? Where is this coming from?"

"I know Jana fucked you up, Lan. I do. But you have got to get yourself together and grow up. Sleeping with anyone in a skirt...skirts that work for us...isn't funny or smart and, frankly, inappropriate as hell for a partner."

My lips form a straight line as I nod my head. "So, it's not just Serena you talk down to then. Good to know. But I'm actually *not* one of your kids, so watch your fucking self."

"Then stop acting childish," he barks.

"You're the one making ridiculous accusations because someone is actually taking an interest in helping *your* daughter become a better lawyer. Trust me, she wishes it were you."

"What the hell does that mean?"

"It means, why the hell did you offer her this internship if you weren't going to show her shit? The whole point is for her to *learn* and you haven't done much except get her to alphabetize your fucking filing cabinet." *She's better than that.*

He stands up, pressing his fists into his desk and glares at me. "Stay the fuck away from my daughter, West."

Too late for that. I'm already addicted to her.

"Whatever it is you have in your head about me aside, don't you think it's about time you start trusting your daughter to make decisions for her life? Why do you have such little faith in her?"

"I have plenty of faith in her."

"No. You treat her with kid gloves. You shield her from the world because you're convinced she can't handle anything. You're too overprotective and it's crippling her."

"Don't talk to me about my daughter like you know anything about her."

"I've observed enough. I've talked to her enough to know how and what she feels. Have you?" I'm officially over this conversation and I know the more I speak, the more my feelings for Serena will begin to shine through. I open the door before he can say anything else but stop on the threshold. "I would never do anything to intentionally hurt you or your family." That is all I have for him. I have no intentions of hurting Serena. *Ever.* Quite frankly, I believe that she is the one with the power to hurt me. While I'm skeptical about forging a relationship with her, I know if I commit to her, I'll be all in.

But what happens when she wants out?

I close the door behind me, letting out a sigh, and reach for my phone that I felt vibrating while I was in his office.

Bambi: I guess no fooling around in your office then. *sad face*

Me: Probably not a good idea now

I stare at my phone for a second. *Fuck, I want to see her. I want to make sure she's okay. And, okay, maybe I also want to put my lips on her. Somewhere, anywhere.*

Me: Meet me in the garage.

Ten minutes, and a short drive to an abandoned lot later, Serena climbs out of her car and into mine. "Hi." Her eyes are warm and she doesn't seem nervous, which makes me feel better.

"Hi back. You okay, Bambs?"

"I'm fine. I'm used to it, honestly. My parents still see me like a child."

"Yes, I gave your father quite the earful over that."

Her eyes widen and she blinks them several times in confusion. "Wait, what?"

"I didn't mean to but...your father..." I sigh. "Serena, he wants me to stay away from you."

A scowl finds her face and for the first time I think I'm seeing an angry Serena Mitchell. "Fuck that." Her hand finds her mouth and a small smile forms behind it. "You're a bad influence on me."

"That seems to be the general consensus," I say, sardonically.

Her face falls. "I was kidding. I don't actually think that."

"I know." I lean across the console, needing a kiss and she happily obliges. She tastes like pumpkin and I briefly wonder if she drinks those trash latte's that every girl I know drinks. It tasted like heaven on her tongue though.

"I don't want to stay away from you," she says against my lips before she backs away and looks around my Benz. "You really lost your virginity in a car?"

I nod, reminded of the fumbling sixteen year old who wasted two condoms trying to get it on before finally getting it right. "Indeed."

"How was it?"

"My first time? Quick." I chuckle.

She giggles and cocks her head to the side as she looks at me. Her nose scrunches, causing her glasses to move. "We'll go slow?"

The implication in her voice makes my dick stiffen. "When the time is right, yes."

"What if that time is…now?"

"Now? Serena, I'm not fucking you in my car for your first time."

"Oh. Right. Blood." She winces. "You have very nice leather seats."

"Fuck the seats, Serena." I could get the car detailed. Quite frankly, the idea of Serena's innocence smeared all over my seats makes my dick hard as granite. "Your first time is not going to be a quickie in a car before we have to go back to work."

"But I'm ready." She pouts.

"No, you're not, you're rebelling."

"What? What does that mean?"

"It means your father just made me even more forbidden than I already was. And you're pissed at your dad, and you want to show him you can do what you want."

"That's what you think this is? Is that how *you* see us? Is that how you see everything that's happened between us?" Her eyes well up with tears and before I even have a chance to take it back one trickles down her cheek and she wipes it away. "Am I like all those other girls?"

"No Serena, of course not." I press my hand to her cheek. It's cool under my warm hand, and only now do I notice that her nose is red. I turn the heat on, hoping to warm her both inside and out, and she presses a kiss to my palm.

"You're not the forbidden fruit. You're just...a guy I like. A guy I like spending time with." I slide my hand down to where hers are folded in her lap and pull her small hand into mine. "I'd seen you in passing from time to time, but the first time you talked to me..." she licks her lips and turns her head to mine, "I felt something. Something I hadn't felt before. It's all happening so much faster than I thought this could happen and it's scary and exciting and I know my dad is going to throw a fit. Probably my mother too. God knows my sister will have a million opinions on the matter, but it doesn't matter to me. It's my life, not my parents or Skyler's. I'm not asking for more than you're willing to give, I swear. This isn't me saying I want to be your girlfriend or anything...I just...I think you're the person I'm supposed to take this step with." She looks up at me. Her eyes are confident and willing, but I can see her nervousness as she prepares for my reaction. She shifts anxiously in her seat and her skirt rises higher, reminding me of just what's underneath it.

"Serena Mitchell, my little Bambi." I run my finger down her cheek, her neck, and down her shoulder. She shudders and I can sense the fire burning beneath her skin.

She wants it.

Hell, so do I.

"Does the offer still stand for me to come over later?"

"If you didn't, I was going to throw you over my shoulder and drag you there myself," I tell her before I press my lips to hers.

The rest of the day is uneventful. Preston stays away from my office, and Serena only walks by my open door a dozen or so times, swinging her hips as she walks by every time. Towards the end of the day, I'm staring at the door, drooling as I wait for another glimpse of her.

Bambi: I'm going to go home and grab my stuff... I assume I can stay over?

Me: Yes. Get your sweet ass to my place now. Drive carefully.

I'm leaving the office when I catch a glimpse of Preston's open door. He usually leaves before I do, wanting to be home for dinner with Viv, but now I have someone waiting to have dinner with *me* too. Jana was hardly ever home when I got there. She was either out shopping or at dinner with friends, or God knows where. More times than not, I came home to an empty house. Griffin would be at a friend's house or after school activities, and then as he got older, out with friends or other social functions. That was when I started staying later and later at the office. Coming home to a house where everyone was already asleep felt a lot less lonely.

Serena *wants* to be there. She wants to be around. I take a few steps towards Preston's office before I shake my head, not wanting anything to ruin my mood before I see Serena.

I'll talk to him tomorrow.

I pick up a bottle of wine on my way home and decide to stop in the florist next door that I used to frequent. *I can't even remember the last time I bought flowers.*

"Good evening, sir!" a short, middle-aged blonde woman chirps from the counter. "What can I get for ya?"

I start to say my regular: twelve long-stemmed red roses when something else catches my eye. I move towards the source of my intrigue and run my finger over a purple rose. Each rose in the arrangement is perfectly bloomed, each petal flawless and full.

"It's the perfect bouquet. I haven't seen one quite like it in a while. Purple roses mean enchantment." She continues.

"The giver seeks to express that they've fallen in love…perhaps at first sight. There's a deep magnetism between the giver and receiver, perhaps something so powerful and profound neither understands."

I scratch my beard as I glance around the room at all the other flowers. None of them say Serena. None of them explain my feelings for her.

Am I falling for her?

Have I already fallen?

Have I fallen in love with her without even having sex with her?

Holy shit, if I'm feeling like this now I'm going to become obsessed the second I fuck her.

Am I ready for this obsession to infiltrate my life?

Am I ready for the end of my friendship with Preston?

The questions are flying at me a mile a minute and the only thing I can think to do is smile. "These. I'll take them." I point at them and hand her my credit card. "All of them."

"All?"

"However many you have. I'll take them all."

She smiles and moves back towards the register. "She's a lucky girl." Her cheeks blush and for the first time, it escapes me that a woman had possibly been flirting with me. *Has she been checking me out this whole time?*

Three hundred dollars and three dozen flowers later, I'm back at my house. I set the vases on the table—Grace, the florist, had surmised that I wouldn't have anything to put these in when she didn't see a ring on my finger. I shoot Serena a text that I'm hopping in the shower, in case she arrives before I'm out. I send her the codes, advising that she park inside my garage this time, to avoid my neighbors' nosy gaze and start stripping out of my clothes.

I don't know how long I'm in the shower, but suddenly

I sense that I'm not alone. I turn my head, slicking my hair back and I see her leaning against the wall in the bathroom staring at me with hungry eyes. "You got here quick," I tell her through the glass door.

She bites her lip as she rakes her gaze over me and then her hands are pulling her top over her head. She sheds the rest of her clothes in lightning speed and then my shower door is open.

And she's in my shower with me.

Naked.

Both of us naked.

Fuck.

"Baby, are you on the pill?" I ask before she can get too close and I officially lose all restraint and the ability to make responsible decisions like keeping my dick out of her pussy.

"No." She pulls her hair down from the ponytail, letting it fall all around her in sexy waves. Her eyes are still on mine and her steps haven't faltered.

I groan the second her hand wraps around my dick. "I want to finish what I started." She looks up at me as she begins to stroke me. "The flowers are beautiful." She smiles. "I assume they're for me?"

"Who else would they be for?" I raise an eyebrow at her and she nods.

"Just checking."

She lowers herself to her knees and wraps her lips around my cock instantly.

Shit, her mouth is incredible.

I begin to push slowly in and out of her, not wanting to push her too far. Our eyes don't break contact once as I begin to thrust into her wanting mouth.

Well, I'll be damned.

I look down and I see one of her hand between her legs and my eyes widen. "Serena, are you…touching yourself?"

Another nod.

The girl that had never touched herself. Never had an orgasm.

"Tell me, does it feel good, baby?" I can see the smile in her eyes. She pulls back briefly. "Not as good as when your tongue is there."

Fuck.

"I need to taste you again. I'll make you come so hard, baby. You know that, right?"

Another nod.

I press my hand to the shower, tangling my other hand in her hair and just as I feel my balls start to tingle, I stop her, knowing what I need more than shooting my seed down her throat.

I want it inside of her.

"I don't want your mouth. Not now. I'm so desperate for you, I can't even think straight."

Her breath hitches and her pupils dilate. "Yes. Yes. Yes. That." She nods her head several times and I don't wait another second. I turn the water off and pull her out of the shower, even foregoing drying off before I have her pinned to the wall of my bedroom. "We're still wet." She giggles.

"I don't give a fuck. I need you and the only wetness I care about is between your fucking legs." I press my lips to hers as I lift her into my arms, letting my cock dig into her stomach after it grazes her sex. Her legs wrap around my waist, opening herself up to me and her scent swirls around me.

"No one has ever bought me flowers before. They are so beautiful," she whimpers between kisses.

"*You* are so beautiful," I tell her. I grip her ass with one hand and weave my hand through her hair as I explore her mouth with my tongue, devouring her delicious moans every few seconds. The water is still sliding down her body and yet the only wetness I'm hyper-aware of is what's smearing across my stomach. I pin her to the wall and back up slightly to grab ahold of my dick. I slide it slowly through her slit, collecting her wetness on my tip. I look up to find her staring down at where I'm touching her, where she's touching me, *where we're connected.* She clenches, and the crown of my dick disappears slightly into her sex and for a second, I think about pushing inside.

I'd only gone raw with Jana, but the idea of doing that with Serena doesn't terrify me like it has with other women. I want it. I *crave* it. I want to feel every inch of her virgin pussy as I rip through her innocence. I want to see the evidence coated on my cock when I pull out of her. But I can't.

I won't.

And I won't put the responsibility on her to make that choice when she is just as needy for this as I am while in this sex haze.

"I need to get a condom. Get on the bed."

"Or…we could do it without one?" she asks, her eyes full of question and wonder.

"Serena," I grit out, my restraint holding on by an actual thread and she grabs my face, pulling me to look at her.

"One time." She holds a finger up. "And you pull out. But…I just want to feel everything."

I eye her, my cock one inch inside a twenty-one year old's pussy as I think about why I'm even contemplating this.

This should be a no-brainer.

My mind is screaming that this is a horrible idea, but my dick's argument is *much* louder.

"I'm clean," I tell her. "I can show—" I start, prepared to let her see my latest test results.

She puts a finger to my lips and shakes her head. "I know you'd never do anything to hurt me."

"Never." I shake my head at her as I carry her over to the bed and lay her down on my Egyptian cotton 1020 thread-count sheets that are currently getting ruined from the wetness of our bodies. I spread her legs, wrapping my hands around her thighs as I sink to the floor, and grip her tightly as my tongue meets her clit.

Fuck. I give in and let myself indulge in her taste, swirling my tongue around her sweet sex. "Landon. Sex. Please." She moans as she pulls me away from her pussy. "You've eaten me out at least six times between yesterday and today."

"What can I say? I love the way you taste." I smile at her.

"And I hope you always feel that way." She giggles. "But right now, I *need* something else."

I stand and she wraps her legs around me, thrusting her hips upwards. I pull back, holding my dick as I prepare to push slowly inside of her. "This is going to hurt a little." *I can't remember the last time I had sex with a virgin, but suddenly I'm nervous as hell.*

What if I really hurt her?

She'll be okay, my subconscious responds.

What if I come too fast?

Likely.

I slip two fingers into my mouth before releasing them and sliding them between her lips. "Suck."

She does eagerly and lets me go with a cheeky pop before her lips are on mine again and she pushes me to my back. "You want to be on top?" I ask her.

She nods as she straddles me, her sex hovering over my dick. I sit up slightly to watch as she wraps her hands around my cock and rubs me through her folds. I'm not penetrating her, she's merely rubbing me against her swollen clit. Her head flutters back, as tiny whimpers escape her mouth and I watch enthralled as the goddess on top of me uses me for her pleasure. Her slick sex wetting my dick is a visual that I won't forget, maybe ever.

"Serena," I manage to whisper, my body holding on by a thread watching her seemingly use my cock to stimulate her clit.

Her head shoots up, her eyes finding mine and those teeth sink into that delicious lip of hers. Fuck, I want to taste them. The need to have her lips on mine is overwhelming every single one of my thoughts.

She slides down my cock inch by inch and I feel that familiar pop as I push through the barrier and then moisture, *everywhere*. "Are you breathing?"

Holy shit, she's tight.

"Yes," she whispers, but I can see the tears forming in her eyes. "It's really intense."

"I know. Breathe, baby." I coach her, although I'm barely breathing myself.

She steadies herself on my chest, curling her hands and pressing her nails into my chest. She pushes herself down the final inch and then I'm filling her completely. Her pussy rests at the base of my cock, and as she stares into my eyes, a look of lust and wonder and something I can't quite put my finger on, I realize I am totally screwed.

"Fuck me, baby."

Eleven

Serena

I GLANCE DOWN BETWEEN US AS I RIDE HIM AND SEE THE TRACES of red on his cock. Surprisingly the streaks of blood don't cause any flares of embarrassment. Feelings of possession bloom in my chest, and I begin to move faster as I ride him. *Mine.*

Every time he looks down at his dick, he'll be reminded of my innocence.

"Fuck, Serena. You're so fucking tight, you're going to make me come."

I whimper in response to his comment. His breaths are becoming more labored and I can tell he's struggling with not unleashing his seed inside of me.

Part of me wants to tell him to go for it. Come inside of me. Make me a woman, completely. I've only recently learned that I have a reckless side and *that* Serena wants to watch Landon's cum stream out of her cunt.

Since when do I use the word cunt?

"Is that what you want?" I look down at him, as I submerge his dick completely inside of me. I rotate my hips and squeeze as hard as I can before raising my eyebrow at him. The angle that we're in has allowed his coarse pubic hair to graze over my clit every few strokes and the feeling sends a jolt of electricity through my body every time. I lean over, letting my breasts hang just out of his lips reach and his pulse flickers in his neck as his hungry eyes feast on my nipples. They flit back to mine just as he grabs my ass and flips us over so I'm on my back.

I lock my legs behind him, just as his thrusts begin to get more aggressive. "Fuck, I want to come inside of you so bad," he whispers against my neck just before he drags his tongue across it. "I can't." He grunts. *"But I will.* Eventually, I will come inside of you. And I'll fill you up. You'll spend an entire day walking around with me inside of you. You'll be so fucking full, it'll drip out of you." He grins against my neck and I feel myself ready to fall over the edge just from his words.

"Landon," I whimper as I fist the sheets on both sides. "Oh my God, I think I'm going to come."

"Fuck. Me too," he growls. "If you come with me inside of you, I'm going to fucking *lose* it."

"Lose it," I groan. In this moment, I think I'm likely to agree to anything so long as he stays inside of me. The orgasm is so close I can taste it.

"I can't," his voice is strained, like the thought of leaving my body pains him. "Baby, I need to pull out."

"No!" I squeeze as hard as I can just as I feel my entire body splintering into a million pieces. My eyes flutter shut and my body begins to soar. A light flashes behind my eyelids and I feel my body begin to shake. *LANDON!* My mind screams, but maybe I screamed it out loud because I vaguely hear him in my ear telling me to say his name again. My clit throbs with need as I shiver and squirm in his arms and find my spectacular release. "Oh God, Landon, I'm coming!"

I finally manage to open my eyes as the orgasm slowly

wanes just in time to watch his cum explode across my stomach. His breath is ragged and his arms are stretched taut on either side of my head, the veins bulging from his muscular arms. I look up into his dark eyes, trailing my gaze down his chest and the smattering of hair, down his happy trail to his dick. The thicket of hair is groomed, yet with so much masculinity, it makes my mouth water. "Landon," I whisper, as my eyes move from his body to mine. My naked body that is covered in a layer of *him*.

"Fuck, Serena. You feel so good, baby." His hands are on me, rubbing his semen into my skin. Hands that are somewhat rough and also smooth rubbing my nipples, pinching them between his fingers and dragging his thumbs over the tips. "You have the most perfect tits, Serena." He shakes them, enthralled by how they move and it's as if he's never seen a pair of breasts before.

A sigh escapes my lips, a high-pitched whimper followed by a squeal as he lifts me into his arms like I weigh no more than a feather. "Let's get you cleaned up." He carries me back into the bathroom and sets me on the counter, the cool marble on my warm ass causing goosebumps to pop up everywhere and I hiss in response. "Cold?" he asks as he starts the bathtub and begins filling it with bubbles. The smell of lavender fills my nostrils and I bite my lip as I watch his muscular form stand over the tub. It makes my sex tingle and reminds me of what's been there and hopefully *what's to come*. Once he's satisfied with the temperature, he crosses the room, his cock slowly rising again as he walks towards me and stands between my legs. "How do you feel?"

"Amazing." I'm sure I have an almost dream-like expression on my face as I think about the fact that I've recently become a woman. "You're incredible," I whisper.

He leans down and kisses my nose gently before he opens my legs. He presses two fingers to his lips before running them through my slit. "So perfect."

He lifts me into his arms and places me in the tub and I hiss as the hot water hits my skin and loosens my muscles. I've barely settled before he slides in behind me and I'm pressed up against his chest and between his legs. He wraps his arms around me and kisses the side of my head. "You're so quiet," I tell him.

"I'm...just letting it all soak in." His fingers find the space between my thighs, rubbing the sore, slick skin and removing the traces of blood.

"What?"

"You. This. Us." He tells me as he peppers kisses on my shoulder and sucks the skin into his mouth.

"There's an...us?" I turn my head, a smile forming on my lips.

"If you want there to be."

I turn in his arms and climb into his lap, so that I'm sitting directly on his cock. "I want," I tell him before I attack his mouth. "I want you so fucking much." I grip the back of his head, slipping my hands through his hair and massaging his scalp. "Fuck me."

His face lights up as he cups mine gently. "You're so beautiful." He tells me as I sink down on his cock again.

An hour, a bottle of wine and a large pizza later, Landon and I are wrapped up in each other on his couch underneath a cashmere blanket, sharing mindless kisses and touches as we watch television.

"How will it be at work?" I rub my nose against his chin and snuggle closer into his embrace.

"You mean besides me going crazy with jealousy when those fuckers look at you?"

I roll my eyes and rub my hand along his thigh in attempts to calm the beast. "No one is looking at me."

"Everyone is looking at you and it drives me insane. Their eyes feasting on you when they think no one is looking. When they think *I'm* not looking. You have no idea how gorgeous you are." His lips find my ear, and he takes it between his teeth.

I smile at his words. "I think you're exaggerating."

"And I think you need to come again. Lie back." I giggle in response as he moves us quickly so that he's hovering over me. "Part your legs," he whispers and reaches under his t-shirt that I happened to be wearing. "You're sore, but not too much for my mouth." He winks at me as he descends down my body, leaving feather kisses in his wake as he makes it to my pussy. He's just about to make contact with my sex when the doorbell rings, followed by three raps. I frown as he sits up looking towards the door and then back at me. "Who the hell could that be?" He crosses the length of the room and peeks his head out of the window and when his head snaps back to look at me, his eyes are wide. "Shit," he whispers. "It's your dad."

"What!" I exclaim.

"Go upstairs. Don't make a sound," he urges as he leads me out of the room before he presses a kiss to my lips. "Don't worry, I'll handle it."

I scramble up the stairs, but I don't go to his room. I sit on the step as I prepare to hear what my dad has to say.

Thank God he had me park in the garage. Imagine if my dad saw my car parked out front.

I hear the door open and his voice floods the room. "Lan."

"P." I hear the door close and a few steps but I believe they're congregated in the foyer and I wonder if it's because Landon didn't hide the two wine glasses sitting on his coffee table or the obvious fact that he isn't alone.

"Staying in tonight?"

"Yep."

"Listen, Landon, about earlier…" I hear a deep sigh. "I was an asshole. I know you'd never hurt my daughter…you'd never be inappropriate with her. I never should have insinuated that you'd do that shit. To us. To Viv…" He trails off and I can't stop the tears from welling in my eyes. I press my hand to my mouth as I think about what it's going to do to my father when he finds out. What it's going to do to Landon and my father's relationship when this comes out.

Would we ever come out?

Landon doesn't say anything and the awkward silence dwells on. I crane my head, thinking maybe they're whispering when I hear my father's voice again. "Okay, well…do you want to go grab a drink, maybe?"

"Actually, now's not a good time." I can't see Landon's face, but I do hear the dismissive tone in his voice.

"Company?" My father asks, and I note the implication.

"Nope. Just doing some work."

"Well, want to watch the game? Pats should be on in an hour."

"P, tonight's not a good night. How about tomorrow?"

"What's with you, man?" he asks. "Come out with me. Are things still going on…with you and," he clears his throat, "Miss Barrett?"

"No," he barks, and I can't ignore the twinge of jealousy that comes from hearing her name. "That's over."

"And she hasn't quit yet, I'm shocked." I hear the lightness in his tone, and I'm sure he has a smile on his face.

"Preston, I'll see you at work tomorrow."

"Alright. Well…" I hear his him trail off and then more silence after a bit of shuffling. "Two wine glasses?"

Fuck.

"Preston…"

"You couldn't just be up front? I would have left. Where'd you meet this one? God, please tell me no one from the firm?"

I don't hear him reply and I wonder if he's shooting him a look because my dad speaks again.

He chuckles. "Alright, alright. I'll see you tomorrow, I guess. Enjoy your night."

The door closes and then I hear Landon coming up the stairs. He turns the corner and then he's kneeling on the stair in front of me. "Serena," he whispers.

"I can't believe he showed up…and he said…he said that you…" A lone tear trickles down my cheek and his thumb wipes away the tear.

"He didn't love the idea of us in his office." I nod and he sits next to me on the step. "So, you know what this means, right, baby?"

"We can't…" I clear my throat, preparing to expel the words from my throat, but I feel them getting caught. "Be together?" The thought is like a jolt of sadness to my heart and, for a second, I swear it skips a beat.

"What?" His eyes snap to mine and his hands find my cheeks. "No…no, God no. I'm not giving you up. I just meant no fooling around at work. We have to be professional." He rests his elbows on his knees and looks at me. "And one day when we decide we're ready, I'll talk to Preston…somehow." He chuckles darkly. "And pray he doesn't kill me."

Over the course of the next month, Landon and I try to maintain a modicum of professionalism and, for the most part, we've kept it together. But there have been a few slips. A few lingering hungry gazes, a hand that grazes down my back when he thinks no one is looking, a chaste kiss to his lips when *I* think no one is looking. But we've laid low for the most part. The only time that he's come close to blowing our cover has been when I get male attention.

I've just stepped out to get some coffee when I sense someone in my periphery. "Serena Mitchell, you're a hard person to see," Justin jokes as he falls into step with me as I walk to the nearby coffee shop.

"Hey, Justin." I smile, and even though we are off the firm premises and not even within sight range of the windows in Landon's office, I swear I can feel his eyes on me. I look up at Justin, and I'll admit he's quite attractive, but he does nothing for me. "What's up?"

"Not much, I've just been preparing like crazy for this hearing on Friday. I don't think I've even slept." He chuckles. "But I was thinking maybe we can get a drink after I have my life back?" We find ourselves at the coffee shop, and he opens the door for me. "After you, Miss Mitchell." The coffee shop looks like your standard hipster, trying so hard not to be a Starbucks complete with exposed brick and colorful loungers.

"Thank you." I smile and, right on time, my phone begins to ring. LW appears on my screen and when I send him to voicemail I realize I also have a text from him.

LW: Didn't I say no coffee?

"Fuck," I whisper under my breath. *How the hell does he know? Does he have like a sixth sense about me?* It's kind of hot, but I wish he understood that he has nothing to worry about. It's him who has me screaming every night. It's him who makes me fall deeper and deeper. It's Landon I'm risking everything for. No man could be a threat to him.

"So, what do you think?"

"About what?" I ask as we make our way through the line to the front.

"Drinks? Or dinner on Friday?"

"Oh." I nod. "Right. That's actually not going to work, I don't think."

"Oh…okay, well maybe some other time?"

"Actually, Justin." I shake my head. "I'm kind of seeing someone." What a lie. If kind of seeing someone is code for being passionately infatuated then, sure, I'm 'kind of' seeing Landon West.

We place our orders and stand idly waiting for our coffees. "A drink is harmless, though. I promise I'll be on my best behavior." He grins as he crosses his heart. A grin I'm sure has worked a thousand times and gotten him a thousand girls, but it doesn't do much for me.

I'm about to answer when I feel a hand wrap around my elbow and tug me towards a wall of muscle. "Serena." Dark brown eyes smile down at me, crinkles forming in the corners and a deep shadow around his mouth that I'd sat on just this morning.

Shit. "Mr. West." I nod and his eyes roam my body lasciviously.

Geeze, Landon can you not do that with an audience? I raise an eyebrow at him in question when Justin interrupts.

"Don't you usually send people out to get your coffee?" Justin asks with a hint of judgment in his voice.

"I decided I needed some fresh air." He gives a smug grin before he turns to me. "Serena, you're needed back in the office."

Translation: get your cute little ass away from this douchebag.

"Of course, just let me just get my coffee." I point at the barista.

Translation: Calm down.

"I'll wait and walk you back," he answers.

Translation: No.

Justin stares at us, like he's an outsider looking in, confused. "Land—"

"I said," he looks at Justin, "I'll walk her back. You're dismissed."

Great.

I shoot Justin an apologetic look as he leaves, his eyes looking back every few seconds towards me, and I wonder if he's putting two and two together.

I *really* hope not.

"Really, Landon?" I say as he drags me by my elbow outside and away from work, further down the street. "Let me go." We turn a corner down a side street and he pushes me against the brick.

"What did I say?"

"I didn't have coffee with him, relax, will you?" I roll my eyes cheekily, glad to indulge in his little game.

"No. I most certainly will not relax, Serena," he snaps. His eyes are so full of heat they're burning and melting my insides. His lips are on mine before I can respond, his tongue almost down my throat with possession, and his hand reaches up my skirt. He pulls away leaving me breathless but keeps his hand between my legs. "Let me give you a little piece of advice. That man wants to fuck you, and if you don't want me to put my fist through his face, I would keep your distance."

"Landon, he d...d...doesn't want me." I stammer, my brain to mouth connectivity slowly short-circuiting as his fingers begin to rub my wet clit. *Fuck.* I turn to the left towards the street. *Anyone could walk by and see Landon with his hand up my skirt.*

"Bullshit. Every man with a working dick wants you and it drives me fucking crazy." He flicks my clit and I all but scream before I throw a hand over my mouth to muffle the cry. "Guys like that are horny fucks that will leave you in a mess of sorrow and STDs if you let them. Is that what you want?"

"No," I reply weakly. Landon has never withheld an orgasm from me before, as it's usually his mission to get me off as much as possible when we're together, but the edge of his tone makes me wonder if he's prepared to leave me hanging at any second.

"Good girl." He coos as he presses his lips to my forehead. He doesn't say anything, as his fingers continue to rub me and dip inside me every few strokes. *God, I'm close.* "No one can touch you, Serena. This special place between your legs is too precious to share with anyone. *Not even me.* But like the silly little doe you are, you gave the lion a taste." His lips are so close to mine, I taste his words before I hear them and they melt me. "And now I can't get enough...I know it's the cliché that a young woman becomes clingy and obsessive to the man that takes her virginity..."

"I'm not clingy..." I blurt out. I understand that he's extremely busy, that I'm not his top priority, and I never asked to be made one.

"I fucking know that, Serena." He grits out. "Sometimes you walk by me in the office without another glance while

I'm all but salivating at the sight of you. Like I didn't rim your ass with two fingers inside of your dripping cunt hours prior. You don't bat an eye when women flirt. You don't react, and it drives me insane. You're so calm and collected. *I'm* the one that's obsessed."

Obsessed. With…me?

"I'm addicted to you." He continues. "To your sounds, your tastes, your looks. Every one of your senses make mine come alive. *You* make me come alive."

"Oh my God." I moan and I don't know if it's his words or the feeling between my legs that cause the reaction.

"God, I need you."

"Now?"

"Yes. I need to be inside of you."

"But we said…"

"I know what we said. But I need you more than I can fucking breathe right now. It makes me crazy that I can't claim you. That I have to watch men hit on you."

"I told Justin that I was seeing someone."

"But not me, you didn't tell him you were seeing *me*."

"Obviously."

"I wish you had."

"No, you don't. You're just being a caveman."

"Your caveman." He growls. I run my tongue over my bottom lip, then my top, my eyes trained on his before dropping to his mouth effectively giving my answer. "My car. Twenty minutes."

Twelve

Serena

IT'S NOVEMBER, WHICH MEANS LANDON AND I ARE GOING ON two months when I decide it might be time to bring up the elephant in the room.

I'm sitting on Landon's couch, my feet resting in his lap as I work on homework and he reads the newspaper when I drop my highlighter into the book and look up at him. "Landon?"

"Yes, dear?" He smiles, but his eyes don't come off the page. He'd gotten a kick out of calling me *dear* in-between his intermittent *Bambis*— *a dad joke if I ever heard one* and I can't ignore the way my heart swells at this particular term of endearment.

My eyes dart around the room nervously, as if how to pose this delicate question will be written on the walls. "Am I ever going to get to meet Griffin?"

He drops the newspaper and looks at me, his perfect features falling as he furrows his brows together. "Of course."

I finger my glasses as I prepare my relentless line of questioning. "When?"

"I figured once you were ready to tell your parents."

"When should we tell them? Tell people?"

"I figured you would let me know?"

"My internship will be over in December, maybe when I'm no longer a permanent fixture in your office."

He leans against the back of the couch and begins to rub my feet, digging his thumbs into the soles and cocks his head at me. "And if we were planning to make you a permanent fixture?"

I fiddle with my glasses again and blink my eyes in rapid succession. "What?"

"We were thinking of having you continue your internship this summer. We know you're going to law school next fall…" He raises an eyebrow at me as if to say, *'and are you ever going to decide where that is?'* "We thought a summer at the firm would be perfect."

"You think me working there this summer while…" I point back and forth between us, "this is going on, is a good idea?"

"What else are you going to do this summer?"

"I was thinking I could intern for another firm?"

He scoffs. "Try again."

"What does that mean?" We are breaking about a hundred rules by being together and it's getting stressful working for the firm where both my father and boyfriend work, not to mention exhausting. My hormones swing faster than a pregnant woman's. If I'm in the room with both of them, I somehow manage to get turned on and annoyed at the same time. *I somehow have to keep my eyes off his dick which is more difficult than one would think.*

"It means I've taken a vested interest in more than just your pussy, Serena Mitchell. You're not going to some far less superior firm for some jackass to derail my teachings. Think again."

After the night my father showed up at Landon's and

apologized, the power struggle between them seemed to wane. My father was more willing to let me tag along with him, and Landon stole me away whenever he could to take me with him wherever he was going. *In a professional manner, of course.* We only made out in his car *after.* Nevertheless, I was learning quite a lot from Landon… *besides the obvious.*

"But Landon…" I can't help the whiny tone my voice takes. *This is a horrible idea.* "I don't want to work there while everyone knows we're together. It'll be so awkward."

"It'll be fine. I'll address your father, Frank, and whoever the fuck else thinks they're entitled to an opinion."

"I hope you approach my father nicer than that." I roll my eyes. "Fine, we can circle back to that later. Griffin?"

"His mother is going to Lake Tahoe this weekend for some retreat, he'll be here then…I was going to talk to you about whether or not you wanted to be here. I know you spend your weekends here…" I'd conveniently started staying with Zoey on the weekends the last several weekends because, *"it was time I put myself out there,"* much to my mother's excitement. I swear my father is still side-eyeing me and is convinced I'm hiding something, but my mother is ready for *bambinos, Bella!*

As in plural.

"Do you think…do you think he'll like me?" I ask, and I immediately regret it. Landon's relationship with his son is in such a precarious position that Landon is convinced most days Griffin doesn't even like *him.*

"He'll love you, Serena. Any issues he may potentially have with you will be about me, not you, baby. He was raised to have impeccable manners, but I think he's forgotten that as of late though."

"I'm not much older than him though…" I trail off. "I don't want him to call me like ma'am or something."

He chuckles and rolls his eyes. "I'll pass along the message."

"Does he know you're seeing someone?"

"No. I haven't seen him since we've gotten serious, and I'm lucky if I can keep him on the phone for five minutes when we talk."

"Are you going to tell him before you introduce us? Don't blindside him, Landon."

"You think that's best?" he asks and my eyes widen in shock.

"What! Yes, of course. What are you going to say? Hey, Griffin, here's my girlfriend, by the way, she's twenty-one?"

"I didn't realize you had an issue with our age difference." He lets go of my feet and immediately I feel guilty for how I phrased it.

"I don't. I definitely don't. But I'm not so naïve to think that other people won't take an issue with it. And forget other people, I'm not so naïve to think that *our* people will be totally on board."

He runs a hand through his hair and stares straight ahead, his eyes fixed on the wall, and before I can decide to give him some space I climb into his lap and wrap my arms around his neck as I snuggle into his chest. "Sorry."

He noticeably relaxes and wraps his arms around me. "Don't be sorry. I'm just...tense about Griff, that's all."

"I get that. And if you're not ready for me to meet him, I'll stay away this weekend. I can survive without you for a few days," I joke.

He tenses below me and pulls my face out of his chest. "I can't."

My heart races as a vision of him telling me those three words flash through my brain. *Does he love me? Is that where this was heading?*

My feelings are getting stronger by the day and it's getting to the point that being away from him is not only difficult but at times unbearable. He has been this unstoppable force that came barging into my life and my heart and I'm realizing that I can't deny how deep my feelings are for him.

The thought is scary. How will my family take it? How will his family take it? What if it ruins what little bit of relationship he has with his son? I'd never forgive myself.

"Not going to *Zoey's* this weekend?" my mother asks. I'm pulling the chocolate souffle out of the oven that I had decided to make on a whim, when I hear her voice behind me. I tap the top slightly and smile when I note that it's perfect.

Okay, maybe I'm on a baking binge because I'm nervous about meeting Griffin tomorrow. I had thought it was a good idea for Landon and his son to spend some time together before I showed up, so I wouldn't be going until the following day.

I turn around after setting it on the counter and look at her. "Why do you say it like that? And why are you looking at me like that?"

"Maybe because I know you. *Sono tua madre, bella.*" I am your mother, Bella. She shoots me a knowing look, that look all moms have perfected that says: *I know you better than you know yourself.*

"I don't know what you're implying."

"*La mia ragazza è innamorata.*" My girl is in love.

"Mama..." I trail off, but there is no lying to my mother or ignoring the physiological reaction that happened from thinking about Landon. I can feel my cheeks heating and

121

without thinking I slide my glasses to the top of my head, a telltale sign that I'm going to start crying.

"Oh, Rena," she says as she makes her way towards me and envelopes me in her arms just as the first few tears start to fall. I hadn't meant to start crying, but the intensity of the past few months coupled with what I know will be *at best*, a rocky few months in the future, causes the tears to form before I can stop them. "What is it, honey? *Cosa c'è che non va.*" *What's wrong?*

I wipe my eyes, knowing that I'm going to have to lie to my mother for perhaps the first time ever. "Nothing, Mama. It's just been a long semester. I'm just stressed about finals."

"Uh huh." She pulls back to look at me and wipes her thumbs under my eyes. I feel like I'm looking into a mirror of the future and it stuns me just how much I look like my mother. Hazel eyes, and hair the color of chestnuts is pulled back into a neat bun. She slides her frames above her head to look at me. "I'm not going to tell you a boy isn't worth your tears, Serena. Love is hard and sometimes there will be tears. Sometimes there will be hard times." She tucks a hair behind my ear and gives me a smile. "Does he feel the same?"

"I'm…I'm not sure." I stammer. "I think so."

"Then you don't give up."

I hadn't expected this reaction from my mother. "This is a very different philosophy than what you preach to Sky."

"Skyler is…impetuous. That's my baby, but she acts quickly and with her whole heart in an instant. You, my first born…" she strokes my cheek, "I see so much of myself in you. You observe everything and absorb it into your soul. You're cautious and you've protected your heart for so long. But I always knew the first man you gave your heart to would be the one."

My scalp prickles as more tears form. *Is Landon the one? Or is my mother projecting her high school sweetheart romance onto me?*

"Mom, I don't know about all that…It's still so new."

She smiles and nods once. "Mmmhmm. Well, I would love to meet this boy that has gotten your interest."

Landon is certainly not a boy. Fairly certain he's older than Mama.

"Soon." I nod. "I promise."

My leg bounces nervously as I sit in the garage, parked next to Landon's car. My nail finds its way into my mouth, a habit I gave up years ago, as I try to calm my racing heartbeat. I know Landon knows I'm here having heard the garage open and close, so I know I'm on borrowed time, but I can't bring myself to move. I turn the car off and finally have the nerve get out when the door opens and I see Landon moving through the garage towards my car. Before I have a chance to open my car door, my passenger side is opening and he's sliding in next to me. "Hi, baby." He smiles and it heats me *everywhere*. He sighs. "Just seeing you makes everything better."

"I feel the same." I return his smile, as I start to wonder if maybe I've been worried over nothing. "I…I was coming in. I just needed a second." I let out a breath. "I'm nervous."

"I missed you last night. Give me a kiss." I hadn't expected that to be his response, but I lean across the console anyway, knowing that his lips on mine would probably calm me better than any deep breathing exercise.

His tongue slips through my parted lips and I sigh into his mouth before I pull back. "I missed you too."

"Griffin is going out to meet some friends soon. Which is

perfect because my mouth has a date with your pussy, and we know you can't be quiet." He winks before he's out of the car.

"Hey!" I purse my lips as he makes his way to my side and opens my door for me.

He kisses my nose and wraps his arms around me. "Don't be nervous."

"'Kay," I whisper. *Easier said than done.*

I follow him inside and I'm not sure what I was expecting—a welcome wagon? —because Griffin is nowhere in sight.

"He's upstairs." I nod in response. *Maybe he doesn't want to meet me? Which is fine; I think I might actually pee my pants right here in the kitchen.*

"Maybe this isn't—" I start when I hear Landon calling up the stairs. "Griff!"

"WHAT?!" I hear screamed back and my eyes widen.

"Can you come down here a sec?"

"Pass."

I notice Landon's jaw tightens and I know he's gritting his teeth. "Let me rephrase that. Downstairs, now."

"Land—" I start. *I don't want him to be forced to meet me.* I try to get his attention when I see a damn near man walking down the stairs with a scowl on his face. He's as tall as his father with hair and eyes almost the exact same color of brown. Sporting a grey sweatshirt with the words *Tigers Football* on it and sweatpants to match, he glares at his father as he passes him. The headphones around his neck are still blasting music. and he has a pencil behind his ear revealing a stud piercing. I hold my hand out, "Hi Griffin, it's really nice to meet you." I give him my warmest smile, but when he doesn't return it, mine falters and my hand drops.

He narrows his eyes slightly. "You know you and I went to the same elementary school?"

"Griffin," Landon speaks through gritted teeth.

"I was in Kindergarten, you were in fifth. I tracked down one of my old yearbooks when dear old Dad told me he had a new girlfriend that was practically my age." He looks me up and down before he rolls his eyes. "You have a younger sister, right? She was a senior when I was a freshman."

Oh God. "Sky-Skyler," I stammer.

He chuckles. "Unreal."

"Okay, enough," Landon says. "Upstairs."

"Fine. I'm out of here, anyway."

"Nice to ummm...meet you?" I choke out as I feel the tears in my throat.

"Be right back." I hear in my ear, followed by a kiss on my cheek, but I'm fairly certain I'm in shock. As soon as Landon leaves the room, I feel myself completely deflate and the tears start streaming down my face.

It's not about you, Serena.

It's not about you.

I chant the words in my head as I realize that while it might not be completely about me, it is about Landon. *A man who has become a part of me.*

A few minutes later, I hear a door slam upstairs and then Landon comes into view as he moves down the stairs. I quickly wipe my eyes before he can see that Griffin's words affected me. He crosses the room and pulls me into his arms, hugging me to his chest. "I'm sorry."

I pull back and put my arms on his chest. "Don't be sorry. I'm the one that should be sorry. I pushed for this...I thought...I mean, this just wasn't the right time."

"There was probably never going to be the *right* time. My son hates me, and you by proxy."

"He doesn't hate you, Landon. Or me. He's just angry.

125

He's upset. He's sixteen." I shrug. "His parents are getting a divorce, he's in legal trouble, he can't take the car when he wants…" I chuckle. "Any kid would be pissed." God knows I want to break down completely, but I want to be strong for Landon. *He needed me to be strong.* Just like I'd need him to be the strong one when we go to my parents.

"Blake's outside, I'm out," I hear grumbled as Griffin walks by the kitchen. I turn my head just in time to see jeans and a hoodie walk by the kitchen and into the foyer.

"Be home by midnight!" Landon calls.

"Whatever." I hear, and I frown as I'm fairly certain at sixteen, my parents would have yanked me back into the house and told me my plans were indefinitely canceled if I ever took that tone with them.

Pink colors his cheeks as if he can hear my thoughts about Griffin's blatant disrespect when my eyes meet his and he backs up a little. "You hungry?"

"Not for food," I tell him as I make my way towards him, unbuttoning my shirt with every step before I let it fall to the floor.

"I know what you're doing." He tells me as he lifts me into his arms and sets me on the counter.

"I'm not doing anything." I lean forward, desperate to make contact with his mouth when he backs away.

"I don't know how long it's going to take for him to come around…" He trails off.

"I don't mind waiting."

"I'm just…really fucking sorry, Serena. I don't know what to do about him." He rests his elbows on the counter and drops his head into his hands.

"Have you thought about seeing someone?"

His head jerks up to look at me. "Like a therapist?"

"There's nothing wrong with needing a little help understanding your child. Most parents don't." I shrug.

He stands up straight and crosses his arms. "What's that about? You think I don't notice those comments you make because I let them go by, but I hear them. Viv and P adore you."

"Is that what you think? Is that what you see? Perception isn't *always* reality, you know."

I shrug, unsure of how to unleash the different kind of daddy issues I have. Not all of them stem from an absent father or one that doesn't pay you any attention. There could be other issues, ones that you don't even realize you have until you're older and the damage is done. Ones that involve another sibling.

"Skyler is the little princess of the family. I was only two when she came around and it was…difficult sharing the spotlight. Mostly because Skyler didn't share, she *took*." I shrug. "So, I grew up being the quiet one, the shy one, the *reserved* one, because Skyler was loud and exuberant and all the attention was always on her, and I don't know," I sigh, "I guess I resented that. Her and I have a weird relationship now. We fight a lot… we *grew up* fighting a lot, and I'm not always the nicest to her. My parents have refereed a lot of our fights over the years and my dad always took Sky's side. It's hard growing up in a house where you don't feel like you're heard, you know?" I had come to terms with this years ago, so I'm almost numb to the feelings about my parents, but exposing this part of my heart to Landon makes me more emotional than usual. I don't even realize I'm crying until I feel his hands under my eyes. "Shit. Sorry."

"Look at you, swearing and everything," he jokes as he presses a kiss to my forehead and laces my hands with his. "Serena, look at me, baby." I meet his gaze. "I hear you. I see… everything about you, even the parts you try to hide."

The butterflies in my stomach explode from their cocoons, fluttering throughout my whole body. "No one has ever...wanted to see." I had spent years guarding my heart, only letting a few people in, but Landon has surged through and planted his little white flag there. Claiming it, marking it, owning it.

He can have it.

"Landon..."

"Serena, I am...so crazy about you. Do you hear me?" He grips my jaw and stares into my eyes. "Crazy. So crazy that I want to tell your dad what's been going on. So crazy that I want to spend Thanksgiving and Christmas with you...wherever that is. So crazy that the idea of you going away to law school has me wanting to pack up my shit and follow you."

I gasp. It had been a thought in the back of my head. *What would happen if I go away?* Pending my LSATs, a few schools have already been sniffing around, including my father's alma mater in D.C. "But you're a partner here. In a huge firm you helped build."

He shrugs. "I can go anywhere, baby. Would I prefer you went to one of the eight states I'm licensed to practice law, that'd be great, but I'm not picky. I just want to be where you are." He smiles and my eyes widen at the implication.

"You've taken EIGHT different Bar exams?"

He snorts. "That's your takeaway?" He shakes his head. "No, only three, but I can waive into the others."

"Right, reciprocity." I scratch my head. "My home is here though."

"Didn't we talk about you moving out for law school?" He points at me and taps my nose. "You need space."

"I know. I don't know where I'll go though. Maybe Zoey will want to live together." I shrug.

"Or you know you can live…with *me?*"

My mouth drops open and, for a moment, I think my brain isn't firing off any synapses because my mind is completely blank. "Like…together?"

"Or not." He backs up, but I slide off the counter and scurry towards the man that is putting his guard back up.

"No! That's not what I meant. I was just surprised that's all. It's really soon and…"

"By the time you graduate and then start law school, it won't be all that soon. It would be about eleven months. My divorce would be final…I don't know." He shrugs. "I thought it might be nice having you around all the time." One side of his mouth quirks up in a smirk and all I want now is to mount him here in the kitchen.

Living together? Like…permanently? Holy shit! "Can…can I think about it?"

"Of course. We have time. I wasn't thinking today."

I nod, my mind still moving a mile a minute at the idea of living with Landon. "I'm considering Yale, you know." I start up the stairs and he follows closely behind, his hand grazing the curve just above my butt with every step.

"I want you to go wherever your heart desires, Serena. And no more of this being afraid shit. You are a big fish, baby." When we get to the top, he presses me against the wall and touches my chest with his pointer finger. "It's time to show the world what you're made of."

"Where are you?" The growl pulls me out of my sleep and I blink my eyes several times to try and chase the remaining slumber away. I turn my head to the side to see Landon rubbing a hand into his eye and sitting up in bed. "Sorry baby, go back to sleep." He murmurs towards me before he gets up and slides his sweatpants over his naked body. "Griffin, it's two in the goddamn morning, where are you? I'm coming to get you. Tell me where you are right now... No, you are not fine, and if you're not walking through this door in thirty-five seconds, you are *really* not going to be fine," he barks into his cell phone.

I sit up as I see him getting dressed and figure I should probably follow suit in case I have to stop Landon from killing Griffin. He snaps his finger at me and points back at the bed, signaling that I needed to get back in it. I shake my head and put my hands on my hips after I've successfully put my leggings and one of his shirts on. I pull my hair into a ponytail and slide my glasses onto my face as I hear him still arguing with Griffin. I follow him down the stairs and when he ends the call he turns around and I can see the torture in his eyes. *I want you with me always, but...maybe not now.* "Baby, can you stay here? I just feel like...that might be best."

"Yes...I mean...will you be okay? I know you're a little worked up and...did he tell you where he is?"

"I have an idea."

"Okay, I'll stay." I reach around him and pull him down to me, planting my lips on his and reminding me of what we did earlier this evening.

"More of that when I get back. Put the alarm on when I leave." He winks and then he's gone.

I make my way back upstairs and climb into bed. I was going to wait downstairs but I thought maybe I'm the last person Griffin wants to see when he gets back, especially if he's already in huge trouble. Skyler used to break curfew all the time and she was never a happy camper when she got caught.

Twenty minutes later, I hear someone come in the door and the alarm blares throughout the house causing me to jump. I sit up, waiting for it to go off, but it doesn't seem to be stopping. In fact, it's getting louder.

I furrow my brow wondering why Landon isn't turning the alarm off when it starts to go faster.

"FUCK!" I hear screamed and I'm off the bed before I can think and bounding down the stairs. I see Griffin pressing every single button on the alarm system and I realize that he must have gotten a ride home by someone that was *not* his father. He sees me and points at the alarm system, a look of panic in his eyes. I punch the code in and he breathes a sigh of relief. "Shit. Thanks."

"How did you get here? Your dad went to look for you."

"I told him I was on my way home, he's such a control freak."

"Kinda what parents do." I shrug, as if to say, *don't I know it.*

"What are you my new one?" He snorts as he walks by me and into the kitchen. He opens the refrigerator and pulls out a beer and my eyes widen.

"Ummm…does your father let you have those?"

"What, you going to tell on me?" he sneers.

He's going to call me step-mommy dearest! "Well…umm… no…or…I don't know? But…"

"Look, first party I ever went to, your sister was teaching us how to shotgun beers, so don't get parental on me."

"I'm not my sister," I tell him.

He shrugs and takes a healthy sip of the beer. "Shame. She seems tight." I try to ignore the flare of jealousy of being compared to my younger sister for the umpteenth time.

"Skyler is the fun one."

"Are…are you drunk?"

"Ding ding ding. We have a winner!" He chuckles as he downs the beer. "This is trash." He scrunches his nose at his father's craft beer. "Of course, his pretentious ass wouldn't have any Bud Light."

"Don't call him that." I sigh, knowing that there's no reasoning with a drunk, angry kid. "I should call your dad and let him know you're home. But maybe, you should go to bed, so he doesn't know you've been drinking."

He laughs and hops on the counter. "You don't get it, do you, Serena? I don't care that my dad knows I'm drunk. He's got a lifetime of making up to do. I think he can overlook my vices that he and my mother damn near caused."

"You shouldn't use that as an excuse for your bad behavior." *Jesus Serena, can you sound anymore preachy?* "I'm not lecturing, I just…"

"Sounds an awful lot like a lecture. Aren't *you* barely old enough to drink?"

"You're not even eighteen, Griffin, and you're already in trouble for underage drinking."

"Ah, but I wasn't driving…" He points at me. *Does he want a medal or something?*

"Which is good, and I'm glad that you got a safe ride home but you should still be more careful. You're being watched and your father is already doing damage control for your future. Don't make it worse."

"You seem like a nice girl, Serena, so I'll give it to you straight. I'm not this asshole kid you think I am. Sure, you don't have the best impression of me right now, but until this year, I rarely acted out. I got good grades, was home by ten, took the trash out without being asked; I did everything my parents asked of me. And then *he* stepped out on us. *He* left." *Wait, what?*

I'm about to interject for clarification when he continues. "My dad thinks I don't know about his *'extra-curricular activities,'* about all the women ready to drop their panties for a weekend at our house in the Hamptons or a shopping spree on his black card." The room spins and I've become very aware at my state of undress as he goes on about all the women that have been in my exact same position. I cross my hands over Landon's shirt as I remember that I'm not wearing a bra underneath.

"He thinks I don't know the real reason my parents are divorcing. Why he was never home when they *actually* were married. Why he moved out..."

"Your father never cheated on your mother, Griffin. He wouldn't—" The words are on the tip of my tongue like word vomit, but Landon would kill me if I spewed the truth all over his emotional son. So, I keep my mouth shut.

"Is that what he told you?" He snorts. "And you believed that?" He stares at me for a beat and looks me up and down, not out of lust or disgust but maybe...*pity?* I hate that. I hate feeling like he feels bad for me when really out of everyone he got the shittiest end of the stick. He's stuck in the middle of his parents' divorce amidst legal trouble and a year of SATs and prepping for college. *I feel bad for him. Junior year is the worst.*

He passes by me, his shoulder grazing mine lightly as he makes his way out of the kitchen before I hear him speak again. "I'm not some delusional kid that's telling you this because I'm hoping my parents will get back together. I'm telling you because Landon West doesn't care about anyone but himself. He breaks hearts. Mine. My mother's. Probably a dozen other chicks...and he'll break yours too."

Thirteen

Landon

THE HOUSE IS QUIET WHEN I GET HOME AND IT TAKES everything out of me not to rock the boat. Had it not been for Serena sleeping soundly, I would have woken Griffin up for round… *whatever*. It's almost three in the morning before I drop into bed next to Serena and pull her warm body towards mine, which to my disappointment is not bare.

"You're not asleep." I murmur in her ear, having known what it means for Serena to be truly asleep. First and foremost, her body melts into mine the second I wrap my arms around her. A sigh usually leaves her lips, and sometimes she turns in her sleep so her head can rest on my chest. So, for her not to move, I know she's awake and furthermore, something's wrong.

"I was close," she says as she turns in my arms. It's dark, so I can't see her face and, for some reason, it worries me.

"How was he when he got home?"

She clears her throat. "Fine." Her voice is raspy and I wonder briefly if she's been crying. *Fuck.*

I move over her and reach for the light on the bedside table. She squints when the area around us is illuminated and my heart constricts in my chest. Just as I thought, her face is red-tinged and her eyes are glassy. "Baby, what happened? Why are you upset?"

"Nothing! I'm not upset, I swear." She shakes her head and reaches for the lamp to turn it off when I grab her hand and bring it to my lips.

"Serena."

"I'm just really tired that's all. It's late." *Lie.* She reaches up and presses a kiss to my lips before she wiggles out of my hold and shrouds the room in darkness again.

She turns on her side away from me, and I stare at her back for I don't know how long before I pull her into my arms and fall into a restless sleep.

A familiar perfume and the smell of mint infiltrate my senses and pulls me from sleep. I manage to open my eyes just as Serena sits next to me on the bed. "Hi, honey." She gives me a sad smile before she presses her lips to mine. "I have to go."

I grab my phone off the nightstand, knowing it has to be early but also knowing she doesn't have class on a fucking *Saturday.* "Why?"

"I have to get to the library. I have an exam before Thanksgiving break and a paper due the week after."

"It's early. Stay. Do it here," I urge her. I can see her shutting down and I want to be there to calm all her fears. *We'd made love while Griffin was gone, and everything was fine when I left. Something fucking happened when I wasn't here.*

"I don't have all the books I need. Landon, it's school." She shakes her head at me like *I'm* the one overreacting and running.

"Baby, if this is about Griff—"

"It's not. But you should talk to him."

"Because that works out so well every time I try? Serena, please don't run from me. I know I have baggage, but..." Jana left me, even before she filed for divorce. She left me the second she let another man stick his dick inside of her. The second she gave her heart and everything else to someone that wasn't me. Since then, I had never gotten close enough to a woman to give them a chance to leave me. But *Serena*...Serena leaving would destroy me.

"That's not what this is about. I really just have to go." I can tell she's still wearing my t-shirt under her jacket and seeing her in my clothes makes me feel like she's taking it as some sort of parting gift.

"Really? Because it feels like you're leaving *me*." I throw the covers off of me and stand up. "What happened?" I raise my voice.

"Can you not yell? It's early and we're not...alone."

"Do you think I give a shit?" I demand.

"You should give a shit, Landon." She snaps, but her eyes tell me she regrets it. She lets out a sigh. "He's your son."

Just as I thought. Definitely about yesterday. "And you're *mine*. He's going to have to accept that."

"Okay." She shrugs sadly and this indifference is starting to piss me the fuck off.

"Why are you being like this?"

"Like what? You're the one throwing a tantrum because I can't stay here all day with you. I have shit to do, Landon!" she snaps and it feels like a punch to the gut. *I have shit to do too. All the time. I just make time for you despite all that.*

"Fine." I'm standing next to the door, refusing to look at her with my arms crossed over my chest as she gets off the bed and makes her way towards me.

She stands in front of me and puts her hands on my arms. "Can I have a kiss?" I don't look at her as I lean forward and press my lips to her forehead, knowing that if I looked into her eyes or kiss her lips I'll probably drop to my knees and beg her to stay. "Okay then."

"Bye Serena."

I'm sitting at the kitchen table, ready for Griffin to make his appearance so we can *talk* about a lot of fucking things when Preston calls me. *God, what now?*

"Hey P." I pinch the bridge of my nose and lean back in my chair.

"Hey, they say the weather is going to get to seventy today. Probably the last warm day of the year. Want to see if I can get a noon tee time?"

No, playing golf with my girlfriend's dad, who didn't actually know I was dating his daughter was not high on my list of priorities. "Actually, I have Griff this weekend," I tell him.

"Oh! Well, maybe you can bring him? How is he doing?"

Besides terrorizing everyone he comes into contact with? Great. "The same as always. I'll see if he's in the mood."

"Make him, Landon. He'll have fun. I'm sure he needs it."

He needs to be grounded forever. "He has plenty of fun, P. Trust me." *Besides, do I trust Griffin to be around Serena's dad right now? God, I could only wonder what he'd extort from me in exchange for his silence once I tell him. Fuck, I need a drink.*

"Alright, well let me know. I just closed the Patterson case yesterday and I need to blow off some steam."

"Well, I'm sure Viv will indulge you." I chuckle.

"We've been *indulging* for two straight days." He laughs and, for the first time since I woke up, a smile finds my face.

"Well, alright, P."

"I feel like I haven't seen you in months. Let's grab a drink next week or something."

"Sounds good," I say as I watch my son drag himself down the stairs with a hood pulled over his head like the classic emo teen. "Listen, let me call you back." I hang up without another word.

"Well, look who's risen from the dead?" To be honest, I want to go straight for the jugular but for a moment I'm reminded of the young boy that followed me everywhere. That wanted to sit on my shoulders everywhere we went. The one that wanted to be me when he grew up. *I miss that kid.*

"Where's New Mom?" He snorts and I'm out of my chair instantly, flinging it back and it hits the refrigerator hard. *Well, that trip down memory lane is way the fuck over.*

"ENOUGH," I roar.

"Whoa relax, Dad. *Joke.*" He puts his hands up, but I can hear the sarcasm in his voice.

"Not funny," I grit out. "What did you say to her last night?"

"Oh, what did she rat me out?" He grabs a water from the refrigerator. "Probably told you I took one of your beers too." He snorts.

"No. But *you* just did. You're SIXTEEN, Griffin. Just who do you think you are? What makes you think you're so grown you can just openly consume alcohol in my house?"

"Oh, now you care?"

"I ALWAYS CARED! What is this shit about me not caring? When have I acted like I didn't care? When have I not shown up for you? WHEN?!" I scream, feeling myself snap after enduring months of his horrible attitude.

"I'm over this." He starts walking out of the kitchen, but I'm in his face before he can make it out.

"We are certainly not finished. You want to live with your

mother? Fine. But you're going to tell me what it is that I did to you that was so horrible that I deserve this shit from you. As far as I'm concerned, there are two people at fault for why this marriage ended. It doesn't all fall on me, Griffin."

"What did Mom do? Besides get tired of waiting around for you to get home? Besides crying herself to sleep every night you didn't?"

"She wasn't crying herself to sleep because I wasn't home, Griffin. *Believe me.* What makes you think you know everything? You're a child. It's not your place to know everything. But, when have I *ever* lied to you? When have I left you stranded anywhere? I'd drop ANYTHING for you, including a job. Something your mother does *not* have. Your mother lied to you, Griffin. I never cheated on her. Why do you think all of a sudden, I'm lying to you? If I tell you I wasn't unfaithful, you should believe that."

"Why would Mom lie to me? You certainly don't make it easy to believe you with the track record you've had before you and mom are even divorced."

"You've got to be kidding me. Griffin, I am your father. I don't owe you an explanation for anything. But just to clear the air, your mother and I are *separated,* and if you're so delusional you don't know the real reason your mother drops you here once a month, then she really does have you brainwashed. As far as *her* lying to you, she's angry at me and she wants to turn you against me and it looks like she's succeeded." He swallows and looks towards the door. I have to count backwards from ten to keep myself from screaming that Jana is the one that cheated on *me.* "I've done everything short of something that could get me disbarred to make things easier with this DUI. I've called in *every* favor in my power, and son, I have a lot of goddamn power. I can't make this go away, not completely."

"It's not about the DUI," he grumbles as he leans against the wall, his anger slowly subsiding into a hurt.

"Then what is this about? Why do you hate me so much? What did I do? How can I fix this?"

He doesn't say anything so I push it a step further. "What did you say to Serena? She means something to me, Griffin. I know you hate me, and you think I'm the root of everything that's wrong in your life, but…Serena makes me happy and she ran out of here this morning like the place was on fire."

"Is that what all this is about? Your toy is mad at you?"

"Watch yourself, Griffin Michael," I scold him. "God, who are you? You're not the boy I raised."

"You're right, I'm not. Must be why you found a new kid to raise." He snorts as he leaves the room, but I don't go after him, because I'm sure if I do, I'll kill him.

And that is definitely a lot of paperwork.

Griffin didn't come out of his room for most of the day. I didn't want him to starve, despite how angry I am with him, so I dropped his favorite from the Chinese takeout place we used to order from in front of his door and went back downstairs to wallow in my self-pity over not talking to Serena all day.

I stare at our conversation from the past four hours that has basically been me just talking to myself.

Me: Hey
Me: Did you make it to the library?
Me: Are you coming back tonight?
Me: Whatever is wrong, we can fix it. Just talk to me.

Me: Why are you so angry at me? What the hell did I do?

I let out a sigh as I toss my phone next to me and put my hand over my eyes. *Why is everyone so angry at me? Have I really put so much bad karma out there?*

Yes, a voice speaks back to me and I scoff. The shit post-separation doesn't count. *What did I do to make Griffin hate me? Why is Serena so pissed?* Yes, I don't have the best track record with women, but that doesn't have shit to do with Griffin. And I worship the ground Serena Mitchell walks on, so what the hell does that have to do with her? She knows she's different.

And you know Griffin said something to her.

My phone pings and I scramble to see if it's Serena, making me feel like a teenage girl. *Who have I become?*

Bambi: Sorry, my phone is on Do Not Disturb when I'm in the library. I'm not angry. I just…I think we're making a mistake.

My heart drops when I read her words.

Me: What? Baby, talk to me. What's this about?
Bambi: I would never ask you to choose me over anything. Griffin, work, your friendship with my dad… those things might be in jeopardy if we stay together.
Me: And you're doing this via text? Are you serious right now?

She doesn't mean it. *You don't mean it, Serena.*

Bambi: I'm sorry, you're right. I can call you when I leave.
Me: I need to see you.
Bambi: I'm at the library.
Me: Leave.
Bambi: I can't…
Me: Then I'm coming there.

A few minutes later, my phone whirls to life and I answer it instantly.

"Landon, don't come here, please," she pleads.

"Why?"

"Because I'm busy."

Busy. I understood busy. I knew the word well. But, coming from her felt like a punch in the gut. "What's going on with us?" She's silent and my heart begins to race. "Serena, I can't do this if you're going to freak out every time someone takes an issue with our relationship. We knew this was going to be difficult. But if we're going to be together, I need you in this with me. Are you?"

She sniffles and I can just picture her with tears in her eyes in her own corner of the library trying to remain quiet. "Landon…I'll call you when I'm leaving the library, okay? I promise."

"Fine," I tell her as I grab my keys and my jacket. The call has barely ended before I'm in the car.

Fourteen

Serena

A WALL OF ANGER COMES CHARGING TOWARDS ME AND MY eyes widen as I take in Landon's aggressive stature. His shoulders are square, his angular jaw—that often looks like it could cut glass—looks like it's ready to slice me in half. He's like a bull and I'm that red cape they wave in front of it, provoking it. Testing it. *Fuck.*

My eyes dart to the guy next to me. Micah, the sweet TA from my senior seminar that doesn't deserve what he's about to witness. The man that's going to get caught in the cross-hairs of this *destruction.* He doesn't see the storm headed our way, as his gaze is cast downward, his highlighter dragging over the words in the textbook, unbeknownst to the murderous glare Landon is giving us. I can hear the sounds of *Clair de Lune* flowing out of his earbuds and I can only hope that Landon keeps his voice down for more reasons than us being in a quiet library.

He stands in front of our table, for a moment, and due to the quiet atmosphere, I swear I can hear his heart pounding in his chest. Despite the weird space we're in, the noise has a direct line with the pounding between my legs. My eyes leave his and immediately go to his crotch, my eyes raking over the bulge growing behind the jeans. I lick my lips, and my teeth find my bottom lip as I try to ignore the feelings of lust coursing through me.

He's extraordinarily gorgeous when he's angry. Wow.

When my eyes find his again, they're softer, as if my lustful gaze has calmed him a little and just like that another feeling spikes inside of me. I swallow, trying to calm the burn in my throat and wishing I hadn't just finished off the last of the water in front of me. I let out a breath, just as his lips mouth one word.

Come.

I stand, not bothering to alert the guy next to me that I'm leaving. I move past Landon, letting the familiar scent surround me, and my senses immediately recognize the smell. My body begins to prepare itself, having affiliated Landon's scent with coming…*a lot.* I feel the moisture between my legs with every step and just when I think I can't get any wetter, I feel his hand at my lower back.

I try to walk faster to pull away from his grasp as we pass rows and rows of books, people sleeping between them, their heads resting on their open books as they prepare for the end of the semester, but his hand only tightens around me.

I pull him into a room, *the stacks,* to be more specific. A small room tucked in the back of all libraries that according to Zoey, was infamous for intermittent study breaks. *Study breaks which were a euphemism for sex.*

The small room is dimly lit, giving the lighting of a scary movie, which is perfect because the look in Landon's brown eyes is absolutely terrifying. Those eyes search my face, his nostrils flaring as he takes deep breaths in and out.

He's pissed.

No shit, Serena! "Landon, I—" His eyes move to my lips,

just as his hands find my neck, stroking my pulse point that quivers every few moments.

"Quiet," he murmurs, as he lowers his lips to ghost along my cheek and down my neck.

I ignore his order, feeling slightly braver than usual. "I asked you not to come here." The bite into my flesh, makes me regret it. "Ow, Landon." I raise my hands to his chest and push back, but his hands are faster, reaching around me and gripping my hips tightly, keeping us pressed against each other. "Landon, stop..."

"No." His eyes squeeze shut as he turns his head away from me, and I wonder if he's trying to hide how angry he is or something else entirely. "Who's the guy?" he grits out as I feel his cock rocking against me and I find myself slowly raising on my tiptoes so that it will rub against my sex and not my navel. "Is *he* why you didn't want me to come? Why you ran out of there this morning? You have a hot study date?" His tone is mocking, but if I'm not mistaken there's a hint of hurt underlying.

"Don't be ridiculous, Landon. He's my teacher's assistant. He's helping me with my paper. A paper I *told you* I had to work on."

"You *left*." He stops his ministrations and backs up to stare at me. He looks like he's at war with himself. "So, you get mad at me, and then hang out with another guy?"

"You know that's not what this is. You're overreacting," I tell him as I raise an eyebrow at him.

"Careful, Bambi. You're on thin fucking ice. I told you, no dinner, no coffee, no other fucking men, Serena. Don't you dare pretend like you think I'd be okay with this," he snarls in a tone so gruff and aggressive I feel my knees buckle slightly.

I straighten and put my hands on my hips. "Landon,

145

we're studying! That is not the same and you know it. I didn't think..."

"Didn't think what? Think I'd be insanely jealous to find you alone with another man? And you claim to have this high IQ." His hands move under my dress and between my legs. It's one of the last of the warm days in Connecticut and I figured I would celebrate the occasion with bare legs under my final dress of the season. *The jury is out on whether this was a good decision or a bad one.* I whimper when his hand makes contact with the waistband of my panties. He snaps the fabric against my skin and I flinch when it ignites a fire between my legs.

"You've ignored me all fucking day. You could barely look at me this morning, and now I show up here and you're with some asshole?"

"You're the only asshole here," I grumble. *Really, Serena, you think poking the beast is going to help?*

I smirk inwardly. *It might.*

"Careful, Serena."

He gets down on one knee in front of me and raises my dress and presses his face to my sex. "I'm going to fuck you here. With my mouth, so you remember just who you fucking belong to. So, you remember that when I say *no other men,* it means *no fucking other men.* Before we leave, you're going to come...*twice,* and then when you've successfully done so, we're going to walk out of here. You will then politely or not so politely, frankly, I couldn't give a fuck either way, tell your little friend that this study date is officially over, and then I'm going to spend the rest of tonight fucking your pretty pussy in my bed."

"Landon..." I whimper as I feel his breath on that slick skin between my thighs. My underwear has already been sent down my legs when he presses his lips to my sex.

It only takes one lick through my folds for me to forget that just this morning I had wanted to put space between us. Space, so that he could figure out things with his son, and space so that I could learn to detach myself from him in preparation for when he inevitably ended things.

Those feelings are long gone.

Landon's mouth on my sex felt like every single one of my nerves were standing on end; a feeling so intense that I can't pinpoint exactly where the source is coming from. It feels like a storm is brewing underneath my skin that is prepared to do significant catastrophic damage. It feels like he's setting me on fire, a full-blown inferno he's started with his tongue.

I can't breathe.

I can't think.

I can't see.

I'm everywhere and nowhere. The feeling is so intense, I can barely muster the strength to speak with the exception of, *"Oh God."* He opens me up even more, bringing my leg to rest over his right shoulder and I hold my dress up so that I can see the scene unfold beneath me. I grab a hold of the steel fixture behind me as I begin to rock against his face, my body building with every flick of his tongue. I turn my face into my arm, biting down hard as I try to quiet the cries leaving my lips.

"Lan—" I moan as I clench and writhe and move with vigor against his perfect face, his beard feeling like tiny spikes on my inner thighs. *A delicious pain that I want to feel over and over again.* Landon has tapped into something I'd never felt ever in my life: a sexual, wanton woman who craves this feeling.

Chases it.

Devours it.

When Landon is feasting on me this way, I'm not the quiet,

timid Serena Mitchell, that plays by the rules. I'm the Goddess, that brought a God to his knees and I'm drunk on that power. The orgasmic high. I'd never felt anything quite like the profound sexual magnetism between Landon and me before.

Physically or mentally.

How can I let this man go?

"*Fuck,* Landon, I'm going to cum," I groan as I feel my left leg begin to quake under the force of the pleasure spreading throughout. His hands grip my ass, holding me steady as his thick tongue licks every inch of my sex before settling on my clit and licking it with such rapid force I feel like I could pass out.

"I love hearing you say *fuck.*"

"*Fuck,*" I repeat. I look down and, in the low lighting of the room, I can see his penetrating gaze looking up at me. "Don't stop." I could swear I heard him say *never* but the words are drowned out by my muffled moans as I fall over the edge. "Oh my God, Landon!" I grip his head and pull him closer as I ride out the rest of my climax. "Fuck me, *please,*" I whisper into the thick sexual haze surrounding us. "Not with your mouth. With your cock. *Please*," I beg.

He flattens his tongue and takes one final lick through my sex before he stands, looming over me.

"What did I tell you was going to happen before we left this room." My body is still hypersensitive as I come down from the mind-numbing orgasm so I'm not prepared when I feel a pinch to the sensitive flesh. I cry out and he swallows my moans with a kiss that is equal parts passionate and possessive. I taste myself on his lips and I'm hungry for more. *So much more.* He pulls away but continues the assault on the space between my legs. "I told you I was going to make you come twice. I want to taste your orgasm again."

"Don't you want to fuck me?" My eyes flutter closed in rapid succession as I bat my lashes, feeding the beast inside of him that wants to devour the innocent deer inside of me.

"That kind of backtalk should have you on your knees," he growls at me, and while I don't doubt he wants my mouth on his cock, the sound of his pants hitting the linoleum floors makes me think I'm about to get my way.

"Legs around my waist, Serena." I obey his order instantly as he hoists me into his arms and presses me against the cool metal of the bookshelf. "Take my dick out." I do as he says and, holding his hard velvety member in my hand, I run my thumb over the tip, collecting the drops of precum.

"Is it for my mouth or my pussy?" I ask him. I stick my tongue out slightly and run it over my thumb, licking his seed from my skin.

He watches the scene, transfixed before he slams his hand against the metal. "Fuck, Serena. When you say shit like that... It's for all of you. Every goddamn drop is for you." He pulls his cock from my hands and pushes through my opening forcefully. *"Everything* is for you." He thrusts hard, and from this position, I feel deliciously full. Like he might drive his cock through me and come out the crown of my head. He freezes and my body starts to panic, wanting his next thrust. "Fuck. I don't have a condom on."

"I don't care," I moan, the lust coursing through me pushing all reason out of my brain.

"Did you take your pill today?" He hasn't thrusted again, and I know he's in agony as we have this conversation.

"Yes." I blush. *Sheesh, you forget to take it like three times and suddenly you have to be reminded.*

It's my first time on any kind of birth control, and since I'm not completely used to taking it every day, Landon makes sure he wraps it up...*most of the time.*

I wrap my arms around his neck and bury my face there, pressing my lips to the skin as he fucks me against the bookshelf with reckless abandon. From the angle we're fucking, every time he thrusts, he hits my clit and that delicious pressure begins to build within.

"Landon!" I moan out just as a bundle of what sounds like encyclopedias come crashing to the ground. "I don't care." I groan, not wanting anything to delay the impending orgasm. "Oh my God, don't stop."

Every time we have sex, I feel like he's teaching me something about myself that I had never known. And evidently, when I'm on the precipice of a soul-shattering orgasm, I'm learning I don't give a fuck about anything around me. I'm fairly certain in this moment, even if the entire staff of the pre-law department walked in, I wouldn't care.

I need him.

I need this.

"Don't you dare hold back on me. Don't you deny me what's mine. Your orgasms are *mine*, Serena. This," he pulls back and thrusts into me again, "is reserved for me." The air around us is thick and I can taste our arousals in the air between us. But I need more. I crash my lips to his, sliding my tongue between his and tasting his tongue. His tongue that tastes like my sex. It's a heady powerful feeling, knowing that I'm all over him. *That he smells like me.* The only time I've ever tasted myself has been on his tongue and *that* is one hell of an aphrodisiac.

"It's yours," I whisper. "It could never be anyone else's."

"You can't fucking leave me. Not after…" He slides me off his dick and slams me back down. "My feelings for you are so fucking *real*, Serena."

If he tells me he loves me, I'm going to fucking lose it.

150

I attack his lips, to prevent him from speaking anymore. It isn't that I don't want to hear it, it's that there is so much we need to discuss. It isn't so simple that we can skip off into the sunset tomorrow. People's feelings are on the line. Relationships are on the line on both sides. Things could end badly and I know the second we say those three words, it will make letting go so much harder.

It's pretty goddamn hard already.

"Don't." His voice snaps me out of my thoughts, and I see his sad gaze on mine as he slows his thrusts.

"Don't stop," I whimper.

"Don't leave me," he whispers. "I can't lose you." I'm so close to the edge I can almost taste it, and he must feel it because he picks up the pace again. Filling me, stretching me, owning me.

I can't leave him.

Leaving him means, I'd lose a part of me.

Is that what all this means?

I can see the storms ahead, but I can fare them if it means I get Landon.

Right?

The answer comes in a flash as familiar tingles flood every inch of my body and I begin to shake under the powerful release. "Oh my God," I cry out as my eyes lose focus and flutter shut. When I open them, my vision is blurry and I feel the tears streaming down my face. "Landon," I whisper.

"Jesus, I love watching you come," he grits out as he continues to chase his climax. "It's like witnessing magic."

"Come inside me. I want to be full...of you," I whimper. I'm very aware of every ridge of his cock as he pumps in and out of me. "I want you to explode inside of me, paint my walls with your cum, Landon. Do it...*now.*"

His hands grip my hips as he pounds mercilessly inside of me, and then he groans out a string of expletives as his cum floods my pussy. I let out a sigh as I watch him fuck me with such determination. His thrusts slow and he sets me onto my feet, pulling my underwear back on and cupping my sex to keep everything *inside*.

My heart is still racing after just having sex, not only in a public place, but *my school library*. "Wow," I whisper, and I look over at him just as he finishes adjusting his pants. He boxes me against the bookshelf that he just fucked me against, his lips so close to mine that I'm breathing in the air he's breathing out.

"I want this. You and me," he whispers.

The tears spring to my eyes and I nod in response. "I do too. It's just…"

"What did Griff say to you?" His voice isn't demanding or harsh. It's calm and soothing and it makes me want to crawl into his lap and stay there forever.

I look down and sigh. "Nothing, I didn't expect. It just re-iterated what I already knew: that I'm just going to be another obstacle in fixing your relationship with him."

"Why don't you let *me* handle that?"

"Because I'm afraid of what you'll do if he asks you to choose."

"What? You think I'll choose you over him and eventually resent you for it when I don't have a relationship with him? I'm a grown man, Serena. I would never blame or resent you for my decisions."

"No. You can't choose me, and that will *break* me." My lip trembles and he presses his thumb to the skin and rubs it gently.

"Serena, no one is choosing anyone." *Sure, he says that now. But what happens when Griffin tells him he'd be interested in reconciling so long as I'm not in the picture.* As if he can hear my words, he continues, "I would never let *anyone* manipulate me. You're a part of my life." He rubs his nose against mine. "A big part of my life." I don't respond to his words because it's easy to say that now. His hands trail up my body and land on my face just before he whispers, "I'm in love with you."

Fifteen

Serena

I CAN'T EVEN IGNORE THE SMILE THAT CROSSES MY FACE AS I watch my sister, Skyler, and her professor turned boyfriend, Aidan, together. They are actually the cutest, and I don't think I've ever seen Skyler so happy and...*settled*. Skyler was this wild, free spirit and Aidan seems to have grounded her. Not to mention, he loves the shit out of her. *Holy hell, is it obvious.* The way he looks at her and touches her like she's the most perfect thing in the world.

It's the way Landon treats me.

I've been on cloud nine since Landon told me he loved me, and it only took me about a millisecond to say it back. A squeal so loud had escaped my lips that I was sure that everyone in the library heard me. I was so in love with Landon West and I wanted to shout it from every rooftop in Connecticut. Now, seeing Skyler and Aidan together out in the open made me want the same. I can't ignore the pang of jealousy that she's able to spend Thanksgiving with him, but I wouldn't be able to see Landon. *He'd be home alone, as a matter of fact.*

I'm sitting on the adjacent couch staring at the movie Skyler put on, mostly to avoid watching them try not to make out, and to avoid staring at my phone to see if Landon is back in Connecticut. He'd been in New York for a conference with my dad for the past two days and I've been climbing the walls to see him, to kiss him, to fuck him. Every part of my body is tense and on high alert in preparation for him to get home, thankful that I already have plans in place to leave as soon as dinner is over so I can see him. I have a date with the love of my life and to *not* be here while Dad grills Aidan on his intentions with his baby.

"Oh girls, your father called." My mother enters the room and pulls the apron off from around her waist as her eyes fall to my sister and Aidan. "Skyler Mitchell, please do not put your father into an early grave," she says as she takes note of their twisted limbs underneath a blanket.

She pulls away from Aidan, whose lips had been planted firmly to her neck and peeks her head up over the top of the couch. "We aren't doing anything! Rena's right here, Mama! But I'll be good, I swear!" She giggles before turning to Aidan and pulling him to his feet. "Let's go to my room."

"*Ripensaci, signorina.*" *Think again, young lady,* my mother warns. "Help your sister set the table." She points at me. "Your father and Mr. West will be here soon."

My eyes dart to the kitchen and my neck snaps so hard I swear I hear it crack. My mouth drops open and then closes and then opens again. Thankfully, Skyler asks my question for me because I am truly at a loss for words.

Skyler's eyes widen and she tucks a highlighted strand behind her ear. "Mr. West? Why is he coming?" She comes to stand next to me as if to shield me from the storm approaching, and for the first time, I really feel like she has my back. I look over at her, the fear from my eyes reflected in hers and she laces her hand with mine.

"Where are your manners, Skyler?" my mother calls from the kitchen. "He's your father's best friend and he's all alone in that house, poor thing. I think that witch of an ex-wife took their son away for the holidays." This is true. Thanksgiving isn't for another week, but Jana decided to take Griffin to her mother's in Chicago for the week leading up to it.

She really is a witch, or rather, something that rhymes with it.

"And he doesn't have like...friends to hang out with? I don't need one of Dad's friends getting him all riled up while he antagonizes my boyfriend." *Nice save.*

"Skyler, you're being dramatic. Now, help your sister," she repeats before she disappears up the stairs and Skyler turns to me with a look of fear that matches mine.

"So, should we start taking shots or what?" she asks.

"I appreciate your votes of confidence," Aidan interjects, as he runs a hand through his dark-brown hair. Objectively, Aidan is a good-looking guy. Being tall, with a muscular build, blue eyes, and the perfect smile, makes Aidan exactly the kind of man Skyler usually goes for, except he isn't a colossal jerk. Based on what she's told me, he is kind and compassionate and understands her better than anyone ever had. *And the best sex of her life.* He continues, "but I think I'll be okay."

"I have complete confidence in you." She wraps her arms around him and presents her lips to him. He accepts with a loud smack causing her to giggle. "But Mr. West...or *Landon,* is Serena's *boyfriend.*"

I blush hearing him being referred to that way. Aidan's brows furrow together slightly. "I thought your mom said he was your father's best friend?"

"Yep," Skyler says as I sink into one of the chairs and put my head in my hands.

As if he's putting two and two together, he nods. "Well,

Serena..." he winces. "Then, I think your sister is right about the shots."

Later that evening, I'm in the guest house getting ready for, perhaps, what may eventually be known as the dinner from hell. I hadn't seen Landon in two days and now he's coming here...to my house...for dinner...with my parents...

This sounds like the worst freaking idea.

Despite my wariness, I still want to look nice, even if Landon can't openly appreciate it. I've pulled on a pair of jeans and an off the shoulder sweater that exposes most of my collarbone and all of my neck. I've pulled my hair off to one side and curled it in tight curls that I shook out to create loose waves—a look I know Landon loves. I'm just putting the finishing touches on my makeup when my phone pings with a text.

LW: I'm sure you've heard the good news?
Me: Aaaand you couldn't get out of it?
LW: Is it so bad that I wanted to see my girl?
Me: In front of my parents? Uh yeah? I haven't seen you in two days! How am I supposed to behave?
LW: Well technically, you've seen...some parts of me *winks*

I smirk and scroll up to our texts from yesterday and I'm met with the most glorious dick in the world. *Okay, I'm totally biased and it's the only one I've ever seen, but I'm convinced.* Last night, I joked that I missed his dick and within minutes he'd sent me a picture.

And it successfully taught me how to masturbate. I guess all I needed was the right material.

Me: Does my dad know?
LW: No. But I think we should tell him...at dinner.
Me: WHAT!? Like...tonight?
My phone chirps again with a text from Skyler

Sky: Bringing tequila over!
Me: No!
Sky: You need to loosen up. Just one...or four.
Me: You are the worst influence, ever! Speaking of which, you taught Landon's son how to shotgun beers?

There's a knock on my front door and then Skyler and Aidan are coming through it. "I don't even know his son!" Skyler chirps.

"Apparently at some party your senior year," I tell her as I make my way into the living area where they have already made themselves at home and are sitting on my couch.

"I mean if he was a freshman, then maybe." She shrugs as she puts two shot glasses on the table. "I was like the freshman Mom; I made sure the guys that were on their sports teams were nice to them. They were like little puppies!"

"Well, thank you for contributing to his delinquency. He has a DUI now, Sky." I put my hands on my hips and look at her over the top of my glasses.

"From the night I allegedly taught him to shotgun? He was like fourteen, what was he doing driving?!" She looks so confused it's almost comical and I wonder if the shots have already taken their toll.

"No, not that night, Sky. Focus!"

"Wait, I'm confused. And baby, slow down," Aidan chimes in and puts a hand over the shot glass she's holding to her lips.

"You're just mad you can't have any."

"Do I want to be drunk at dinner with your parents the first time I meet your father? Absolutely not. And your mother is already side-eyeing me after she caught me feeling you up in the kitchen."

"Oh, she is not."

"But let's circle back to the first thing. He has a son old enough to...drive?" Neither of us say anything and I just blink my eyes several times at him. "I just assumed he was...a younger guy and best friend was another word for like *mentee*. He's, like, *your dad's* age?"

"Do you want to stay in my good graces or no, Professor Sleeps-With-Students?" I'm half joking, but he needs to reign in the judgment if he wants a prayer at keeping me on his side.

Skyler snorts into her shot and shakes her head. "Hey, that's 'Professor Sleeps-With-Student'! Not plural!"

Aidan shakes his head. "I didn't mean anything by that I swear, I just didn't realize...I mean..."

"Don't listen to Serena, our Dad is going to freak." *Gee thanks, Sky.* "But Serena, you've been the perfect child your whole life. It's about time you took a walk on the wild side. Join me, it's fun!" She holds her shot glass up and downs another one.

This was going to be the furthest thing from fun.

We are back over at the main house when a car door slams, sending me flying almost a foot into the air. "Will you relax? I'll try and keep the spotlight on me and Aidan, but you have got to keep it together, Rena," Skyler whispers and I nod, suddenly wishing that I had indulged in at least one drink to calm my nerves. My father walks through the door with Landon in tow, and immediately my body reacts to his close proximity.

Settle down, Serena, now is really not the time.

My father enters the living room first and immediately spots Skyler. *Of course.* "Skyler Alexandra, get over here troublemaker," he teases, with perhaps the biggest smile on his face.

"Dad!" She hops to her feet and bolts for him, letting him envelop her in a hug and kiss the top of her head. *If there was ever any doubt that she's the favorite, it's solidified in that moment.* I don't think anyone even notices me until I look up and notice Landon staring straight at me. His face doesn't give much away, but I hear his thoughts as loud as I hear my own.

Hi baby, I missed you.

I give him a small smile as I stand to approach my dad. "Long time no see, Dad," I joke. I get it to an extent; he hasn't seen Skyler in three months whereas he's seen me almost every day of the last three. But still, I would like just maybe even a quarter of the enthusiasm.

"Hi, sweetheart. Hold down the fort while I was gone?" He kisses my forehead and pulls me into a hug.

It's something.

"Yep, Mom and I had fun."

"So, I hear." He turns back to Skyler. "And I heard you've been having quite a lot of fun in D.C." He raises an eyebrow and looks at the man lingering behind us. "Preston Mitchell." He takes a step forward and holds his hand out to meet Aidan.

Confident and calm, Aidan reaches his hand forward. "Aidan Reed. It's nice to meet you, sir. I've heard a lot of great things about you, both from Skyler and at CGU. Your name comes up quite often." He smiles and nods his head respect-fully.

"Uh huh, my sources tell me you're a teacher there. A *doctor,* if I'm not mistaken."

"Dad..." Skyler shoots him a look and he shoots her one back.

"Skyler?" *Don't start,* his eyes warn.

She rolls her own eyes and goes to stand next to Aidan. "Not after this semester."

"Mmmhmm. Well, I have quite a few questions for you two, but I want to see your mother, and I need to check my messages. Seems I got a bunch while we were in the air." He pulls his tie off and reaches for his luggage. "Lan, make your-self at home," he says before he's up the stairs.

After a few moments, Skyler smiles and bounces in place. "Hi!" She scurries towards Landon and wraps her arms around him. "I'm Skyler. I know we've met in passing a few times, but I'm glad to officially meet you." She backs away after a beat and I know for a fact Landon is definitely overwhelmed. "I'm the cooler sister," she giggles.

"I don't know, your sister is pretty cool." He winks at me, and I smile in return.

"This is Aidan, my boyfriend." Skyler beams up at him as the two men shake hands and I swear I'm the only person who doesn't find this totally strange.

"Okay, as cute as all of this is, what are you doing here? Can't we just stick to the initial plan that was me coming over later?"

He shakes his head as he moves closer to me, his eyes hun-gry and pinning me to my spot, making me shiver with need. "Your dad asked and I had no reason to say no." He looks over his shoulder towards the master staircase briefly before his hands find my face. "Hi, beautiful." His lips press against mine so sweet and gentle it makes me melt. When I pull back, my face is bright red as I remember that we aren't alone in the room. "Landon…" I fiddle nervously with my glasses and gesture towards Aidan and my sister, and she scoffs.

"You literally watched us make out for an hour."

"I didn't watch, but you two need a hose turned on you."

You're one to talk, Serena.

"Come on, let's go, honey. Evidently, they need *privacy,*" she tells Aidan as they head towards the den that is just off the main living area.

"God, I missed you." The crinkles form around his eyes and his smile makes me feel like warm honey is moving through my veins. When Landon's eyes are on me, I feel cherished and special and loved, more so than I ever have in my life. "And I missed your pussy," he growls in my ear. "I've been starved for you and the chance to see you was too tempting to pass up, even if I have to behave." He brushes his nose against my neck and inhales. "I hate sleeping without you, by the way," he murmurs in my ear.

"Me too."

"Have you given any thought to living with me next year?"

My eyes widen and I look around the room, trying to alert him of our surroundings in the off chance he forgot that we are in my parents' living room. "Landon, now is *really* not the time."

"Later." He kisses me again and his tongue begins to probe my lips demanding access when I hear a loud bang and someone barreling fast down the stairs. *What the?* I pull away from him instantly and wipe my mouth, grateful that I had foregone lipstick tonight.

"ARE YOU OUT OF YOUR FUCKING MIND?!" my

father roars as he makes his way towards us, and instinctively, though my father would never lay a hand on me, Landon steps in front of me, shielding me from his wrath.

Oh shit. What? How? I look around the room for a second wondering if they've installed cameras I didn't know about and they saw us kissing.

"P—" My father looks absolutely murderous and his level of anger shocks me.

"Dad…" Skyler appears back in the room, probably having heard what was about to go down.

"Skyler, go." He points at the door. "You and Aidan, go somewhere." He points at the door.

Skyler looks at me, and I nod at her, letting her know we'd be okay, and she mouths *I'm sorry.*

My father's face is bright red, his blonde hair sticking straight up as his heavy breathing slows before he takes a step towards us. "Get away from her, Landon. So, help me *God,* I will put a fist through your face."

He doesn't move. "Listen, Preston, we should talk."

"Oh, *fuck* no, you son of a bitch. The time for talking is *way* over. I told you to stay away from my daughter." His voice is laced with venom and I shiver, hearing him speak so angrily.

"How did you even find out?" Landon's voice is even, but I can hear the nerves.

"Seems your son slipped up to Jana. She called and left me a hysterical message. Viv is certainly beside herself at the news, but she's having it out with Jana right now." *Good, give her hell, Mama!* "And while I relish in the karma for your ex-wife, I am *not* pleased to hear that it regards MY DAUGHTER! I warned you. TWO MONTHS AGO! I told you to stay away from her!" he roars as he points a finger in Landon's face before he shoves him with two hands, hard, forcing him backwards.

"Dad!" I move out of the way just in time but Landon's head still jerks in search of me thinking I'm behind him. The relief is all over his face before he turns back to my father and I'm shocked he doesn't retaliate. "You don't understand!" I plead as I try to stand between them to prevent things from getting physical.

"No, Serena. *You* don't understand. I told you what kind of man he is. How naive can you be that you don't see what I'm telling you is true? Or is *everyone* in the office just full of shit? I know you hear the gossip."

"Preston, enough," Landon barks. "And don't talk to her like that."

"Are you telling me how to talk to my own daughter? Are you crazy? Get the hell out of my house, Landon. And if you think for one second I'm not going to the board over this, think again. We have rules in place for a reason. To protect our staff from predators like you. From men who just have no regard for the goddamn rules! I should have reported this shit after the first and the second and the fucking tenth! I just never thought you'd go after Serena. I never would have brought her around you."

"Dad, it's not like that! I love him." The tears begin streaming down my face before I can stop them, and I'm not sure if they're out of anger or sadness or a volatile combination of the two, but before I can stop them I feel arms around me.

"Don't you dare touch her."

"Back off, Preston," Landon snaps and, in this moment, I'm certain if my father made a move to remove me from Landon's arms, he'd regret it. "Baby, it's okay," he murmurs in my ear and it does nothing but make me cry harder. He kisses my forehead and hugs me tighter and I can't even look at my dad.

"I am not standing for this. Landon, OUT!" he screams.

"I'm going with him," I tell my dad as Landon releases me from his arms, much to my reluctance. *His arms around me are the only way I'll make it through this nightmare.*

"The hell you are."

"Yes, I am! You're not going to tell me who I can or can't be with. You can't tell me who I can love!" I shake my head and reach for Landon, wrapping my hand in his and I squeeze it hard, my stomach flutters when I feel him squeeze back.

"Serena, you don't know anything about love. He's going to break your heart."

"Maybe he will!" I scream back.

"I would never," I hear from my right and when I look over, his face looks tortured and confused like he can't believe I'd actually think he would hurt me.

"I just mean, we don't know what the future holds," I sniffle.

"Yes, we do. You, me, babies," he tells me so honestly that it makes my heart skip a beat.

My breath hitches and fresh tears spring to my eyes as I look at him. "You want...to have a baby with me?"

"*Babies* as in plural," he smiles at me, "and I want them all to look like you." I'm so stunned I can't speak, but my heart is screaming with happiness. The happiness is brought to a halt when my father speaks again.

"Haven't you screwed up enough children to last a lifetime?" My dad sneers and my head snaps towards him angrily.

Too fucking far.

"How dare you!" I exclaim and I am officially *livid.* "That is way over the line."

"Serena, it's okay," Landon says, and when I look at him I see the devastation on his face.

"It is certainly *not* okay. Dad, I'm twenty-one years old and until now when have I ever showed an interest in *anyone?* When have I gone out on dates, or brought anyone home? And believe me, guys showed interest. I'd just never met anyone that...I wanted. I don't expect you to be jumping for joy over it, but I don't expect for you to act...like this." My lip trembles, and suddenly I feel everything pouring out of me. "This is just the standard in this family. Skyler has been doing crazy shit her whole life and the one time I don't toe the line it's the end of the world. The standards aren't the same and it's ridiculous."

"This is way different and you know it, Serena. He's old enough to be your father!"

"So, what!" I scream. "I love him. And *for once*, I just need you on my side. You don't have to support us, just support *me.*"

"What the hell does that mean? I'm always on your side, Serena."

"Are you?" I shake my head. *Now isn't the time to unleash all the issues I have with my father, especially with Skyler more than likely in the next room.*

"You think..." My nostrils flare, as the tears flow down my cheeks more aggressively. "You have no faith in me. No faith to make my own decision. No faith in me as a future lawyer..."

"That's not true, Serena! I just want to protect you."

"I don't need protection!" I scream, and despite the years of pent-up hurt I have built inside, it's as if I can't get the words out. "I don't need protection from *Landon.*"

Landon's hands stroke my back and I wonder if my dad is going to lose it again, but he just shakes his head. "I want you out of my house," he says quietly. "I can't believe you did this.

To me, to my family, to Viv. I never dreamed we'd be having this conversation. Even with all your indiscretions...I thought you had more respect for me than that." He rubs his forehead and backs out of the room. "Just get out, Landon." He points at me. "And you stay here," he says as he stomps out of the room.

The tears are flying fast down my cheeks the second he's gone and turn to full on sobs. "I'm so sorry." I hiccup. "I'm so embarrassed."

"Shhh, don't be sorry." He presses a kiss to my forehead and then my lips that are already starting to swell from the tears.

He wipes my face, but new tears form just as quickly. "Please don't hate me."

"You know that's not even possible. But I do think you should stay here."

"What?" *Is he telling me this is it? No, that's impossible. He just insinuated that he wants me knocked up for the better part of my twenties.*

"Stay here, you don't want things to get worse."

"What could be worse than us not being together right now. I want to be wherever you are."

He smiles. "I love you," he whispers. "Just give your dad a second to cool off."

My lip wobbles and I sink my teeth into it to try and prevent more tears from falling, but it's no use. "When can I see you?"

"You tell me, okay? The second you can." He winces. "I need to do some damage control in case he really does go to the board."

"You're not going to be in trouble, are you? At work?" *They wouldn't fire him, right?*

"You let me worry about that, alright?"

I nod and swallow to try and prevent the words from falling from my lips, but the anxiety bubbles to the surface. "This isn't the end of you and me...is it?"

He cocks his head to the side and gives me a smile that doesn't reach his eyes. "Serena, I've learned so much from you in the past three months. So much about myself and I wonder if that's because you're actually a part of me. A soul knows no age, Serena, and mine recognized something in you instantly. Before I even touched you, I was drawn to you so inexplicably. There could *never* be an end of us." He kisses my forehead. "I'll call you," he tells me and then he's gone.

I press a hand over my heart as I hear the door close and drop to my knees instantly, feeling my heart shatter into pieces spectacularly in response to his eerie words. Under normal circumstances, I would have swooned over them, but he hadn't exactly answered my question, and that broke my heart.

Sixteen

Landon

I'M FEELING A MYRIAD OF EMOTIONS AS I PULL AWAY FROM MY best friend's house which just so happens to also be the love of my life's house. I'm so angry I can barely see straight. Furious. Devastated. Livid.

All the while, I feel so unsettled with what would happen between me and Serena. And I knew just who to take that out on.

Her voice blares through the phone like nails on a chalkboard, and if I had the power, I'd reach through the phone and strangle her. "I was wondering when I'd hear from you," she sneers.

"Are you fucking kidding me, Jana? Do you just enjoy hurting people and ruining their lives, is that it? You're so miserable and unhappy with yourself that you have to make sure others are as well? Misery really does love company, I guess."

"*I* enjoy hurting people? You are sleeping with Preston's daughter! His twenty-one year old daughter! Did you think he was just going to be *okay* with that?"

"IT WASN'T YOUR BUSINESS TO TELL HIM!" I bellow into the phone. "Why the hell didn't you come to me? I could have explained to you—"

"Explained what, that Griff was lying? That you didn't have that skank around my son?"

"Watch your fucking mouth, Jana. Serena is far from a skank. And you of all people don't have any room to talk about promiscuity."

She scoffs. "Fuck off, Landon."

"You do realize that if Preston goes to the board and I get disbarred for morality or ethics, you can go ahead and kiss your pretty little alimony check you're gunning for, goodbye."

The other side is silent and I shake my head. *Didn't think about that shit, did you?* Not that it's totally true. There are quite a few loopholes; the main one being that Serena doesn't technically "work" for our firm, and I plan to use that if it comes down to it. But my guess is that the board won't really give a shit that I'm having a relationship with Serena Mitchell. I make the firm too much money for that.

Preston will certainly give a shit though, and his opinion matters more to me than anyone on the board.

"Jana, I've never wronged you. Maybe I could have been home more, but that was *after* you cheated on me. I was hurt and angry and I could barely look at you. Maybe we should have tried therapy, but I just didn't have it in me. So, I checked out. Maybe I spent too long punishing you for what you did, maybe I took my coldness too far, but you are in the wrong here, Jana. For you to turn our son against me, to go after my best friend…and for your information, *Jana*," I spit out her name and it tastes awful coming out, "I'm in love with Serena Mitchell. Maybe that offends you or her father or whoever else, but frankly soon to be ex-wife of mine, I don't give a damn. And if you don't set our son straight and stop feeding him lies, then I'm going to tell him what actually happened in our marriage. And unlike you, I've actually got *proof*," I growl.

It's true, I have pictures and phone records and an email exchange that highlights all of Jana's indiscretions that I'd kept for insurance purposes.

Stay one step ahead of your opponent.

"You wouldn't dare!" she screams. "And Griffin doesn't believe anything you have to say!"

"Because you lied to him!" I yell. "Jana, I—" My words are halted by the sound of a horn, blaring long and hard, someone slamming on their breaks, and tires screeching against the pavement. My head snaps to my right just in time to see a car connect with my passenger side, hard. I drop my phone just as the car connects and it's like the entire crash is happening in slow motion. The glass of my passenger side window shatters and glass begins to fly throughout the car and I shield my face as best as I can to prevent lacerations. The force of the crash slams me against my driver's side door and the whiplash from my seat belt burns against my neck almost cutting into the flesh. Every light on my dashboard lights up, and every sound imaginable beeps as smoke begins to expel from my hood.

"Fuck." I cough as I lean back against my headrest, trying to gain enough strength to get out of the car. My heart is racing a mile a minute, but my vision is getting foggy and everything sounds muffled. I feel something wet—blood, I think fleetingly—trickle down the side of my face and I try my best to wipe it, but my limbs feel like they're being weighed down by cement blocks, preventing me from moving. My eyelids are getting heavy and the sight of Serena's sweet face is the last thing I see before my eyes shut.

"Mr. West, can you hear me?" Words are being shouted all around me, and I hear the sound of a siren somewhere in the distance. "Mr. West if you can hear me, squeeze my hand. You're going to be fine, sir, but can you open your eyes?" The sensation of being lifted takes over, and then I am set on my back on something hard and stiff. My guess is on one of those boards to keep you straight. My head is throbbing, the pounding behind my eyes so aggressive I think I could pass out at any second. "Stay awake for us, sir. Can you tell us your first name?"

Landon. I don't know if I say it, or merely think it as the sky disappears and is replaced with fluorescent lighting and the ceiling of the ambulance.

I need my phone. I need to call Serena. She'll worry or she'll think I'm ignoring her.

I cough, forcing my lungs to take a breath, and I lift my arms, trying to press my hand to my chest.

"Don't move, we need to make sure nothing is broken and you don't have a concussion. The less you move the better."

"Ser...ena," I manage to force the words out of my mouth, only coughing once in-between. "Call," I whisper and the EMT nods.

"Okay, is that...your wife? Someone else in your family?"

"Gi—girlfriend."

"Okay, Serena?"

I try my best to nod, but I don't think my head is moving. "Tell her..." My voice seems to be coming back, but my body feels like it's getting weaker by the second. "Tell her...I love her."

"You can tell her yourself, sir. Everything is going to be fine. I know you feel a little banged up, but you will feel better when you get to the hospital."

"Tell P, I'm sorry," I murmur, and it's the last thing I remember before I'm out again.

Serena

I was seconds from hopping in my car and driving to Landon's when there's an aggressive knock on my door.

"Go away!" I scream at the only person who would knock like that. I told Skyler to give me some space, but mostly I don't want to stare at her and Aidan and be witness to how easy their relationship is. My dad will give Aidan a hard time for a day or two and that'll be it. He'll accept Aidan.

Will my father ever accept me and Landon?

Will he ever completely accept me?

My door opens and I watch as my parents enter the guest house. My mother, who is always happy and cheerful and rarely has a reason to shed a tear unless she is overwhelmingly happy, looks like she's been crying for the better part of the past hour. Her eyes are red and swollen and she's not wearing her glasses—probably because they got in the way of how much she has been rubbing her eyes. That's why my glasses are perched firmly on top of my head.

"Oh, my sweet Bella," my mother says as she sits next to me and pulls me into her arms.

The feeling of her arms around me makes the dam burst, yet again, and suddenly the uncontrollable sobs erupt out of me. "It's not fair!"

"Sweetheart...you know your dad is just trying to do what's best for you."

"Don't you get that he's what's best for me?" I look at my mother, as she hadn't heard my pleas earlier. "I'm in love with him, Mama. You told me you understood. You said you knew the first man I gave my heart to would be the one."

"Vivianna, you knew?" my father asks, with a confused

expression, and I can tell he's trying his best to keep from sounding accusatory. I've never heard my father take any kind of tone ever with my mother.

She shoots my father a glare before turning back to me. "Baby, I didn't know the details. I didn't know…" She rubs her eyes. "It broke my heart hearing you cry like that." She tightens her hold around me and looks at my father again. "You apologize, right now."

He unfolds his arms and sits on the coffee table in front of me. "How…?"

"That's not an apology, Preston Mitchell," she scolds.

"I want to know how it started." He looks at my mother.

"It doesn't matter. Someone tells you they're in love. *Their first love.* The normal response is *not* to scream at them. You forget it wasn't all that long ago, that my parents weren't too keen about the non-Italian boy I brought home at eighteen." She narrows her eyes at him. "*And* you weren't Catholic."

"Vivi…*it's*…"

"Not different, Preston. Love is…*love.*"

I should have expected this from my mother. This level of understanding is something that only a mother can have and it makes me feel less alone.

"You understand why I reacted the way I did, don't you?" He runs a hand through his hair and rests his elbows on his knees. "I feel like he's taking advantage of you."

"And when I made it clear that was definitely *not* the case, you should have backed off."

"He's old enough to be…" He clears his throat. "He's my age, Serena."

"Technically you've got a few years on him." I point at him. "He would want me to point that out." *I know it isn't the time for the joke, but having my mother here feels like I'm protected from anything my father can throw at me.*

"Serena…"

"I don't know, Dad. It just…happened. I didn't plan for it. But I didn't hide from it either. It just feels right. It feels natural. I know he has a track record, Dad. Thank you for pointing that out." My lips form a straight line as I try to ignore the sinking feeling that, while Landon is my first, there is quite a long line of women that came before me.

He wants you to be his last, though.

"Please don't go to your board. Don't get him in trouble. I'm done interning as of next month, and I don't have to return next semester."

"Your father isn't going to report anything." My mother gives him a stern look and his shoulders sink.

"I was angry and I…I am angry…but…I don't want to hurt you. And some of the things you said, I…it seems like I've hurt you quite a bit."

I shrug. I don't want to get into this. *At least not without a certified therapist present.* "I'm used to it."

"You *shouldn't* be used to it," my mother speaks up. "Sweetheart, I wish you would have said something. We love you and your sister equally. Do you understand that?" Her hands have found my face and she gives me a kiss on my nose.

"I know…*you* do," I respond as I look at my mom. My mom and I are almost one in the same and she's never made me feel like I was less than *anyone.*

"Serena…" My father grabs my hand and holds it between his. "I've loved you your whole life. I'm sorry we haven't had the best relationship, but I hope you don't think it's because I don't love you or I don't care. I thought you interning at the firm would bring us closer together…"

"I thought so too, but... I rarely saw you."

"I know. It was...a shitty few months. I'm sorry, Serena. I am so sorry."

I nod, not knowing what to say. I hadn't anticipated this level of humility and vulnerability from my dad when he knocked on the door, but when I look up at my mom and she gives me a subtle wink, I should have known better.

My mother is always in my corner, even when I don't know she's there.

"Listen about Landon...I can't promise, that I'm going to just suddenly be okay with it—"

"And that's fine," my mother interrupts. "The point is we're going to put forth the effort to be there for you and support your decisions as a grown woman. You are wise beyond your years, Serena, and we are sorry if we ever took that for granted." She tucks some hair behind my ear and kisses my cheek.

The tears have formed in my eyes but haven't made their way down my face, so my vision is blurry, and I wipe my eyes for the hundredth time. But these tears are the cathartic release that I've needed my entire life and certainly after the stressful last three months. I knew eventually we were going to have to come clean, and my father's potential reaction had been weighing heavily on my mind.

But now everything is out in the open.

No more hiding.

No more secrets.

We are free.

Seventeen

Serena

IT'S BEEN ABOUT TWENTY MINUTES SINCE MY PARENTS LEFT, AND I frown when Landon's phone goes to voicemail again. Normally, I'm not one to leave messages, but I don't want him doing anything reckless like setting his career on fire, and my texts aren't going through.

"Hi, it's me...I'm not sure why your phone is off, but I'm going to come over. I talked to my parents, and I just...I want to see you. My dad isn't going to say anything to anyone at work, so don't...think you have to do damage control or take any preventative measures. Please call me though, okay? I love you."

Why would his phone be off? He has a car charger. A shiver runs down my spine as I fear the worst but immediately shake my head.

Landon is fine.

But then, where is he?

I hop in the shower, in hopes to scrub the day off me as much as possible, and when I get out, I immediately pull my hair up into a wet bun. I forego any makeup and slip my glasses on before pulling on jeans and a UConn hoodie. I grab my purse and collect a few things that I don't already have at

Landon's and open the door to the guest house where I almost run right into Skyler on the way to my car. "Hey, what are you doing? Where's Aidan?"

"Oh, he…went to check out of his hotel." I look behind her and notice Dad standing in front of his car.

"Cool, you guys going somewhere? I'm going to go to Landon's, so feel free to shack up at my place. Just change the sheets." I giggle as I think about Skyler and Aidan definitely wanting privacy and to be able to do what they want without fear of our parents hearing them.

"No, Rena…Landon's ex-wife called…*again.*" A solemn expression crosses her face and she looks like she's about to deliver bad news.

"Ugh." I scoff. "What does she want now? Hasn't she done enough damage for the day? God, give it a rest." I sigh. "You know what? I don't care what she said. She's a bitter bitch that's going to end up alone."

"No, Rena…she's still listed as his emergency contact…" Tears flood her eyes, and for Skyler to be crying, that is big.

"Oh my God. What…what happened?"

"There was an accident and from what she told Dad, he's okay…" I see her mouth moving, but all I hear is white noise. My ears are ringing so loudly and I'm suddenly freezing, and I wonder if I'm going into shock, but then my feet are propelling me forward. "Come on, Rena, Dad is going to take us to the hospital."

The entire ride is a blur. I'm only vaguely aware that Skyler is sitting next to me in the backseat and her hand is clasped with mine. She rests her head on my shoulder and squeezes my hand as we take our exit. "I'm sorry you hate me, Rena. I know we have our issues, but I love you so much, even though we drive each other crazy. You're the only sister I've got."

I look down as we pull into the hospital parking lot. "I don't hate you, Skyler. And Landon has shown me that I have so much love to give. I've blamed you for things that aren't your fault and I'm sorry. I love you, little sister." I squeeze her once and then I'm out of the car before it's fully in park, moving towards the entrance. I sprint for the receptionist's desk the second I'm through the revolving doors. "Landon West... he...car accident." I swallow as I try to get my words together.

"Are you family?" She looks down at her file and then up at me.

"Ummm no...I..." I stammer. *They're not going to let me see him?* I almost break down into a fit of sobs, prepared to beg when I feel my father's hand on my shoulder.

"He advised the EMT's on the scene to contact Serena, my daughter. Due to restrictions on his phone, they probably couldn't retrieve her number and could only get his emergency contacts which would be one, Jana West, his soon to be ex-wife. She's out of the state, and contacted myself, his lawyer." My dad's lawyer mode speaks volumes. *He's trying to help, Serena.*

Good. If he hadn't thrown Landon out...

Don't go there. It's not his fault.

"Right, okay." She looks down at her files. "Take the elevator to the fourth floor and push through two sets of double doors. You'll see a nurse's station just off to the left. Someone there will be able to help you."

The ride to the fourth floor and the walk through the hospital halls seem like almost an eternity before I see the nurse's station. "Hi, please," I plead, "I don't want the runaround. I just want to see my boyfriend...Landon West. Is he here?"

"Oh yes, are you Serena? Please tell me you are." The nurse, who reminds me of my grandma—short, with glasses that hang around her neck and silver curls that would make her a shoo-in for a *Golden Girls* remake—grabs my hand as I nod my head. "My, look how pretty you are."

"Th—thank you," I stammer. "Is he…"

"He's going to be fine, honey." She pats my hand and looks at Skyler and my father. "You two can wait here. I'm going to take his girl back to see him now."

"Can you tell me what happened?" I ask as I wipe my nose on my sweatshirt. It's only now that I remember how I'm dressed and that I probably look like I'm twelve years old. *Great.*

"A car collided with his passenger side door. The other car ran a stop sign, but I think Mr. West was on the phone. You kids and these phones, I swear. He's going to be just fine, dear. He's awake, and although he has a mild concussion he's not exhibiting most of the usual signs. He's a little tired and weak but that's normal. He's got some cuts and bruises, but nothing your kisses won't fix." She rubs my arm, giving me a warm smile, and I half expect her to send me in with some tea and cookies. "He's been asking for you since he got here."

"Thank you." I give her a hug, surprising even myself, and make my way into the private room. He turns his head to meet my eyes instantly, and I run towards the bed. "Oh my God." There's a bandage covering most of his forehead and purple bruising surrounding his right eye. He has a few cuts on his cheek and chin and I note bandages on his neck and on both arms but other than that he looks perfect.

"Well, aren't you a sight for sore eyes."

"Don't you ever do this to me again!" I grab his hand and pull it to my cheek before placing a kiss on his knuckles.

"Come here and give me a real kiss." I let his hand drop and I press my lips to his gently. "Hey, why are you crying? I'm okay, see?"

I nod. "You just scared me. I thought…" The tears begin to flow down my cheeks and I put a hand over my eyes after sliding my glasses to the top of my head.

"I'm not going anywhere, baby. Never. How did you get here? I hope you didn't drive. Did Skyler?"

"I didn't drive. My dad brought me and Skyler both. They're outside."

"Your dad brought you?"

"Yeah, a lot has happened since you left." I let my eyes drift down his body. "Clearly," I whisper. "We talked and…he'll come around." I press my hands to his chest and rub it softly. "I'm so sorry." I hiccup.

His hand rests over mine. "Hey, why are you sorry? Come on, give me a smile. You look so beautiful." He raises his arm up slightly in an attempt to touch me before he winces and I know the panic is all over my face. "Don't look at me like that, I'm okay. Just a little sore."

"Well, stop moving around!"

He chuckles. "I was beginning to wonder how I was going to get you here. They told me they could only call my emergency contact." He sighs and shuts his eyes briefly. "I can't wait to be divorced."

"Yeah, me either."

He shoots me a cocky grin. "Eager to marry me, huh, Bambs?"

I feel my cheeks heat up and I press my hands to them to cool the skin. "That's not what…I meant…I just…"

"It's what *I* meant." He reaches for my hand and brushes his lips over my knuckles. "I'm eager to wife *you* up."

"I wouldn't mind being married to you." I smile. "You know, for all the babies you want."

"I'm taking that as a verbally binding contract." He winks. "You're stuck with me now, Mitchell."

The tears start to fall again at this informal proposal and the words fall from my lips. "Best news I've heard all day."

I haven't left Landon's side since I arrived, and at some point, Aidan came to collect Skyler, and my dad had left as well, telling Landon that they would talk as soon as he was out. I've pulled the couch towards his bed and he frowns when I sit down. "Get your ass up here," he says as he slides over. "I need to kiss on you some more."

"No, I don't want to hurt you. You can barely move your arms without wincing. I'm just going to stay here."

He pouts and it's the cutest thing ever. I'm about to give in to his want—*that also happens to be my want*—when his phone begins to ring. I grab it from where it's charging on the table and hold it up. "It's a Facetime from Griffin."

"Wow, I'm shocked."

"Have you talked to him?"

"Nope."

"He just wants to make sure you're okay, I'm sure. Jana did call my dad. They do care about you."

"Give me the phone. He's probably calling to yell at me and tell me I'm a shitty dad."

"Landon…" I hand it to him and go to make my way out of the room to give them some privacy when I hear his voice. "Hold it." I turn around to look at him and he shakes his head. "Stay. Please."

I nod and take a seat on the couch away from the phone camera's line of sight. "Hey, Griff."

"Dad?"

"How's it going, Son? How's Chicago?" Landon asks, but

I know his heart isn't in it. Months of indifference and disrespect and hurtful comments and the past several hours have all culminated to this moment, and who knows what meds they have him on that would make him over this conversation already.

There's silence on the other end. "Dad, I'm really sorry. I really...I mean, I know you think I'm just making this up, but I didn't mean to slip up to mom about Serena. I might be a lot of things, but I'm not a snitch." I watch as Landon cracks a small smile and it warms my heart that he loves Griffin so unconditionally.

He's going to make the best father.

His eyes meet mine over the phone like he can hear my thoughts and I blink away.

Stop looking at him like you're ready to start now!

"Are you okay?"

"I'll be fine." Landon nods.

"Of course, you will. You're Superdad. Remember, I used to call you that?"

"Yeah, it's been a while." He says sadly.

"I've always thought you were Superdad."

"Hasn't felt like it as of late."

"I know. I just...kinda messed up I guess."

"I was sixteen once too, I get it."

"Look, I was thinking that maybe...you know, when I get back, we can hang out or something?"

I smile, hearing his words.

"I would really like that, Griff."

"Alright, cool. I love you, Dad."

He narrows his eyes slightly and I think it's because he's trying to keep from getting emotional. "I love you too, Son."

"Alright, I'll text you later."

He nods before disconnecting the call. "Pretty sure he hasn't told me he loved me in over a year."

"You gotta start somewhere." He nods, and I know this conversation is far from over, but he changes it anyway.

"So, when are you breaking me out of here? It'll be three days since I've been inside of you and I am *not* pleased."

"Whenever the doctor says we're free to go. We are not escaping just because you want to get your dick wet."

"I love when you talk about my dick. Say something else." He winks and slowly rubs his dick.

"No, because you don't know how to behave!"

"Come here, Serena." In an instant I'm pressed against him, having been convinced to snuggle against him in bed. He sits up, and I'm on my side, hovering over his. "You're the best thing that ever happened to me, you know that? I'm going to spend the rest of my life trying to make you as happy as you've made me."

"You do make me so happy, Landon. I love you so much."

"I love you too."

I close my eyes slowly, letting the anxiety and stresses of the past day just float away. Landon is fine, and we are both on the road to repairing our respective relationships. A part of me wonders if it had not been for him, would I have ever talked to my dad about things that had bothered me? Would Landon and Griffin ever have gotten their relationship back? Or would Griffin have grown up resenting his father? It makes me grateful that I met this man that taught me to ask for what I want. To go after what I want even if it's scary as hell. Because in the end, it's all worth it.

The exhaustion has fully kicked in and just as I'm on the precipice of sleep, I hear his words floating around me. "Serena?"

"Hmmm?" I mumble.

"Wanna fool around?"

Epilogue

Landon

Six Months Later

THERE SHE IS.

I chuckle to myself watching her stand on her chair and wave to us wildly with her friend Zoey. There are at least three thousand chairs set up in the field of the University of Connecticut stadium and they're standing up on two of them making them tower over the sea of people. A large stage and podium has been set up in front of them in preparation for the commencement ceremony. Preston and Skyler and Viv are probably the loudest in our section as the three of them are on their feet waving back and cheering for her. Aidan's younger sister is graduating college today also, so he couldn't be here, but I'm sure he'll show up within the next few days because he can only go so long without seeing Skyler.

I know the feeling quite well.

Serena's eyes flit down the row to me and she blows a kiss at me before my phone starts to vibrate. "Hey, you."

"Hi," she giggles. I lean forward slightly, to adjust myself as her voice is already making me hard. She's still standing up on her chair and now she's bouncing slightly. "I might have had a few mimosas since I last saw you."

"How many is a few?"

"Enough that I want to fuck you. *Now.*" I look up at her family next to me who are still taking pictures of their daughter and sister, unbeknownst to them that she is seconds from initiating phone sex with me.

"Serena."

"Come on, don't be such a prude."

"Oh, we're playing that game, huh?"

"I'm not wearing panties under my dress, Landon."

"Fuck," I grumble. "If we miss commencement, your parents are going to kill us."

"Come find me after? The pre-law college graduation isn't until three."

"Deal."

"Lose my family."

I snort. "Obviously," I tell her as I hang up the phone.

"Holy shit, the line for the bathroom was insane," my son says as he makes his way through the row and plops down next to me.

"Don't say shit." He snorts as he looks at Serena, who is finally taking a seat in her chair. "Just think you'll be up there, soon."

"Scary."

"No, you got it."

"I think I'm going to start getting scouted in the fall. You'll be around, right?"

I look at him curiously. "Of course, why wouldn't I be?"

"I don't know, planning a wedding, honeymoon…I figured you'll be really busy next year." He shrugs and I smile thinking about the ring in my pocket that I'm dying to get on Serena's finger.

"Never too busy for you, Griff." I tell him and he smiles up at me and for a brief second, I'm transported back to a time when he always looked up to me like that.

We are getting there though.

"You've seen the ring?" Preston interrupts as he finally sits back down in his seat next to me.

"I was there when he picked it out." Griffin smiles, and I'm glad to hear the pride in his voice.

Until Skyler stomped all over it.

"Excuse me." She pokes her head up and leans towards us. "*I* was there when he picked it out. You got round two." She smiles at us and I resist the urge to flip off my kind-hearted but royal pain in the ass future sister-in-law.

"You couldn't just let me have it, could you?" Griffin jokes.

"Pipe down both of you," Preston says. "It doesn't make a difference if *I* didn't give the okay."

Viv snorts from the other side of Skyler. "Yeah okay, dear."

Preston shoots her a fake glare, and I wonder how in the world I ended up in this crazy family with what seems to be all the love in the world. Griffin and I have had several extremely long talks about my relationship with Serena, including how he would feel if she moved in, and he seems to be completely on board. It's as if my relationship with my son made a complete one-eighty and I couldn't be happier to rebuild some of what we lost.

"I can't believe my big sister is getting married!" Skyler cheers.

I can't believe it either. I never imagined that three months after my divorce was finalized I'd be rushing to get back down the aisle again. But I'm ready. I'm ready to make her Serena West and then quite possibly a thousand little Wests.

Hopefully, Griffin is on board with that idea as well.

Brown hair and blue polyester come charging for me and then she's in my arms with her legs wrapped around my waist, pressing dozens of kisses to my face. *Yep, I can smell the champagne, alright.*

"Bambi, how much did you have to drink?"

"I don't know. Zoey just kept pouring them."

I rub my nose against hers as she climbs out of my arms. "Come walk with me for a second."

She doesn't follow, and when I turn to look at her I see her hands on her cocked hips. "Are you asking me to marry you?"

I freeze, wondering how in the hell she knows, and then I let out a laugh because she knows *me*. That's how she knows. I hadn't planned on it right this second. I had plans to do it after dinner, right before I took her home and ravaged her until the sun rose, but the words tumble out of my mouth before I can think. "Yeah, I am. Is that okay with you?"

She nods as the tears spring to her eyes and she fiddles with her glasses. "Absolutely."

I'm vaguely aware that we are on a football field surrounded by thousands of people, but I grab her hand and bring it to my lips. "You have been the best surprise of my life. The twist in the second act that I didn't see coming. I want to spend the rest of my life discovering that magic I feel when I look in your eyes. You are the love of my life, Serena Mitchell, and I want to be married to you for the rest of it. Will you marry me?"

The End.

Author's Note

Thank you so much for reading! I hope you enjoyed reading about Landon and his baby deer, and a small glimpse of Skyler and Aidan! Serena's story started forming in my head as I was writing about her sister and I definitely didn't see it shaping up into this story. But I'm so happy with the way it turned out! The next campus tale will be out early next year, and it'll be my first that's based on true events! (Not mine, I swear!) As always, thanks for going on this crazy ride with me! Onto the next!

Acknowledgments

Carmel Rhodes: My sounding board! The person who reads every version of every story I write including the copy that is basically just stream of consciousness with no punctuation and the shortest hand possible. Thank you for talking everything out with me no matter what time (and talking me off the ledge) and most importantly for becoming a night owl like me as of recent. No clue what I'd do without you. So much love.

My Beta Baes: Helen Hadjia, Kristene Bernabe, Leslie Middleton, Melissa Spence, Erica Marselas Thank you for seeing my magic even when I don't. For being a team that cheers loud, supports louder and loves my characters the hardest. You made this story even better and I value your feedback so much. I'm a better writer having all of you in my corner.

Jeanette: Thank you for another kick ass cover! (And everything else that comes with it!) Thank you for knowing my vision before I'm even sure what it is.

Danielle James: I love our chats! Thank you for always letting me pick your brain and encouraging my bad habits like making teasers before a book is done! Thank you for giving me real, honest and laugh out loud feedback.

Vera Finotti: My Italian tutor! Thank you for all of your help on both First and Second Semester! *Sei il migliore—You're the* *best.* (I didn't check with you to make sure this was correct, so hopefully it is!)

Kristen Breanne and Stacey Blake: Thank you for making my books so pretty time and time again! I'm so confident sending my book babies out into the world knowing you've worked your magic!

My author friends: Thank you for always being so supportive and sharing my stuff and being on this journey with me! You guys are the real MVPs.

To everyone in the Hive and all of the Witches: You guys make me laugh on the bad days, smile harder on the good days, and believe in myself every other day in between! You're amazing and I love you!

And finally, to the readers: Thank you for taking a chance on my books, I hope you enjoyed it!

About the Author

Write. Wine. Work. Repeat. A look inside the mind of a not so ex-party girl's escape from her crazy life. Hailing from the Nation's Capital, Q.B. Tyler, spends her days constructing her "happily ever afters" with a twist. Romantic comedies served with a side of smut and most importantly the love story that develops despite inconvenient circumstances.

Sign up for her newsletter (http://eepurl.com/doT8EL) to stay in touch!
Qbtyler03@gmail.com

Facebook: .facebook.com/author.qbtyler

Reader Group: www.facebook.com/groups/784082448468154

Goodreads: www.goodreads.com/author/show/17506935.Q_B_Tyler

Instagram: www.instagram.com/author.qbtyler

Wordpress: qbtyler.wordpress.com

Other Works

My Best Friend's Sister

Bittersweet Surrender

Bittersweet Addiction

Spring Semester

First Semester

Unconditional

Forget Me Not

Printed in Poland
by Amazon Fulfillment
Poland Sp. z o.o., Wrocław

37032305R00114